BOOK ON

Him and I

MELIA A

This is a work of fiction. Names, characters, places, and incidents either are the product of the author's imagination or are used fictitiously. Any resemblance to actual persons, living or dead, events, or locales is entirely coincidental.

Copyright © 2022 by Melia A.

All rights reserved. No part of this book may be reproduced or used in any manner without written permission of the copyright owner except for the use of quotations in a book review. For more information, address: Meliiaa_A@outlook.com.

First edition published and printed in May 2022.

Cover Design by Emma Mallory
Edited by Kriti Tripathi

ISBN 979-8-4425-2685-1 (paperback)
ISBN 979-8-8031-4829-6 (hardcover)

"The one person she least expected to count on, was the only one there in the end."

Him and I

Him and I

Prologue

Was it shame or was it the truth finally being set free? I have never felt so free and so alive as I did now. Yet, there are always consequences to your actions. I wasn't ashamed because it was finally out in the open. I was ashamed that I didn't know my true self and what I had to do to get here.

But how could something so wrong. . . feel so good at the same time? This is not what I asked for, but here it is now.

"Put the gun down, Scott."

I clung to the wall, watching it all unfold in front of my eyes. Hunter was standing there with no hint of emotion in his eyes while the barrel of the gun was inches from his face. Did I do this? Did one moment manage to change everything that I knew? And was it worth it? Kaiden's hand was shaking and one could see the rage in his eyes as tears fought their way out.

"You were my best friend! Was this your plan all along?" He yelled out.

But how was Hunter so calm? Like it wasn't the first time with a gun in his face. I was terrified for him.

"What the hell are you talking about?" Hunter asked, sounding slightly annoyed.

I wanted to move or just say something, but the shock took over my body and I somewhat felt numb.

"Admit it!" Kaiden yelled again.

He cocked the gun, leaving just a soft touch before it fires. Why wasn't Hunter reacting?!

"Be careful with the gun, Scott. One wrong move and someone could get hurt."

With a quick movement, Kaiden suddenly had his arm on Hunter's chest and the gun on his face. I looked at him with shock and fear. I'd never seen him like this before. I had to do something. But what could I possibly do?

"Shoot me, go ahead. And make sure you don't miss. Because if you do. . ." Hunter grunted, "you earn an enemy and you should know you don't want me as one."

No one ever prepared me for any of this. If I could give myself one piece of advice from all that I've learned. I'd tell myself. *"Don't let two men fall in love with you. . . It won't end well. . ."*

Chapter 1

Two Months Earlier

Beep... Beep... Beep...

I rolled over, grabbing my phone to shut the damn thing off. Another day to make it through. But today wasn't just any regular day. It was the day I finally became an adult. I quickly put on my school uniform and rushed down to the kitchen, and just like clockwork, so did my brother. It happened to be his birthday too because we are twins.

"HAPPY BIRTHDAY!" My parents said in sync.

There was a cookie cake on the kitchen table with letters spread across it. I've been counting down the days because I was finally an adult and it was a step toward the future. I've worked so hard to get to where I am today, and I couldn't be prouder of myself for that.

"We are finally 18, heck yeah!" I cheered.

My brother and I high-fived, and at the same time, a wave of joy washed over me. The energy was so intense, it made me want to dance. But that's just who I was. Hailey Davis. And next to me, I have my brother Brandon and my lovely parents, Chantelle and Liam. The best parents that anyone could ask for. Their story is pretty complicated, but they worked so hard to give us the life that we deserve.

"What the fuck are you doing?"

Oh, and that would be my bitter-ass sister. I don't understand where the competition came from. As kids, we were really close, but the older we got, the further apart we grew.

"Alyssa, watch your language. We didn't raise you to speak that way." My mom said.

She went ahead, grabbed an apple, and gave me a dirty look. It wasn't toward our brother or anyone else, for that matter, just me. It pretty much felt like my own little sister had become my enemy. It doesn't matter what I do or say. She's just pissed all the time.

"Yeah, whatever. I can't believe I am related to her when she acts like a fool."

I rolled my eyes at her. I wanted to slap that apple out of her hand, but I wasn't going to let her get to me. Because the more I react, the more she enjoys.

"Looks like someone woke up on the wrong side of the bed, even when you're blessed to be related to someone as savage as me." I forced a fake smile.

Maybe the high road wasn't for me. What was the fun in that? The way her eyes twitched any time I said something kind of this brought me some joy. I don't understand what I did for her to resent me, but I was too old for this.

"If you're a savage, then I'm a queen." She laughed before leaving the kitchen.

I'm sure that was her trying to be smart, but I've learned to tune her out. I've worked so hard to get where I am, and I wouldn't let anyone or anything bring me down. I am months away from graduating at the top of my class, and afterward, I can choose from any college I want. So, what was there to be mad about? People might think I have gotten everything handed to me when they see me. But in fact, I've worked my butt off just to make sure I would make it through high school and be able to get into the best college. Sadly, everyone saw me as nerdy and introverted, but that wasn't much of an insult to me. If anything, they told the truth. Yeah, partying and going out are fun, but you can't put that on a college resume. I had to lose a lot in order to earn a lot, and I wasn't sure if they were regrets or really just blessings in disguise. I was too young to commit to anything when I hadn't even finished school yet. But soon, I wouldn't have to put my entire focus on it.

I made my way to school full of everything you know is there. The mean girls, the nobodies, the jokes. And then there was me. I wouldn't say I was the most popular, but I didn't have issues with anyone. I got along with everyone and they just left me alone. But some would say that's me being modest.

"Seriously, can you two get a room? I want to walk through the halls without vomiting."

My brother's locker and my locker were right next to each other, so I never failed to see him with his tongue so far down his girlfriend's throat.

"Good morning to you too, Hailey, and happy birthday, by the way." Diora chirped.

I thanked her and smiled. She was a really stunning girl. She had beautiful dark skin with these brown chocolate eyes and a new hairstyle each day. She was a good girl for my brother, and he was happy, so that's all that mattered to me.

"I can't wait to show you your birthday present tonight." She said and wrapped her arms around my brother's neck.

I faked throwing up in my locker to show them how disgusted I felt about overhearing this. They went back to making out, and here I was reminded that I was forever alone. I mean, it's not like I didn't want to be with anyone. It's just that I don't have the time right now, and there hasn't really been anyone that caught my attention. I actually had that once, and it felt like I would never get it back.

"Sup, losers!"

My locker slammed shut, and it scared the crap out of me. I held my hand to my chest, trying to stop the shock that went through my body. She let out a laugh and Brandon just rolled his eyes. My best friend Luna isn't most people's favorite person. She was rude, selfish, pushy, and your typical popular mean girl. She tries to pull that shit with me sometimes too, but usually, I just brush it off. Because every time she argues with me, her voice turns into this high-pitched nasal ringing, and I can't listen to that, so I just let her talk and get away with things.

"Luna, what did I tell you about sneaking up on me like that? It's too early for this."

I sighed and opened my locker while she laughed at me being scared. Sometimes, I wonder if she thinks that half the things she does are cute or what?

"Yeah yeah, whatever. Did you ask your dad about the party yet?"

"What party?" Brandon interjected.

I felt guilty because it slipped my mind. I was too busy studying.

"Guess. Why else would I be mentioning a party? Especially today." Luna said.

I watched them bicker back and forth until it started annoying me.

My brother isn't her huge fan either. He says she has her head so far up her ass that with her fake lips, it's hard for her to take it out enough to realize she isn't all that. She is a special case, but she is also my best friend.

"I was going to ask Dad if we could celebrate our birthday at his club tomorrow night. It just slipped my mind for a reason."

It probably would have been a good idea that I told him, but it was too late now.

"We? No thanks! I'd rather do something fun with my girlfriend than watch everyone make a fool of themselves there."

"You know he won't agree to it unless you're there, too. Come on, don't bail on me."

I walked up to him and put my hands together, begging him to come. Or at least, that he would tell our dad that he would be there too, but he wasn't budging at all.

"Bail on what? And did someone say party?" Zane interrupted.

I swear it's like anytime someone says the word party, they pop out of the blue. Zane is my brother's best friend, by the way. And I didn't mind him that much, but Luna couldn't stand him. He was basically a male version of her, so it made sense why she couldn't stand him. He was flirty with no filter, but I think deep down, she liked it because it boosted her already high ego.

"Seriously, Zane, do you ever mind your own business? Can you just please crawl back to the hole you came from?"

"You mean the same hole that you came from?"

I couldn't stop myself from laughing hard. It didn't matter what she said, he always had a good comeback that was funnier. At some point, I just kind of blanked while they went at it. It was a morning routine, but today I was without my ice coffee.

"Just ask Dad. I'm sure he'll say yes if he's there."

I stopped and looked at Brandon like he has got to be kidding me. I love my dad, but he was also very overprotective, and frankly, he would ruin the entire mood by being there.

"I wouldn't mind your sexy ass dad being there. If anything, he would be the highlight of my night."

I gave Luna a dirty look because she knew how much I hated it when she talked about my dad that way. Whenever she stays over at my place, she drools every time he is around and rolls her eyes whenever she sees my mom with him. As if my dad would ever go for someone like her.

"You better keep an eye on her. One day she might throw herself at him because she is that desperate." Zane said, laughing.

This entire conversation made my stomach turn. They argued again until the school bell started ringing, and I couldn't have been happier because that meant I could get away from this awkward situation. I don't like any kind of drama. It's so draining, and I don't have time for that. This was the reason no one had any problems with me, because I always walked away from any situation that distracted me from my goals. Because if you think about it, once you get older, all this petty high school drama won't even be important. So, I'd rather keep my head down and focus on accomplishing my goals instead.

Chapter 2

Finally, lunch came around and I headed to the football field to wait for Luna. As I said before, she is your typical popular girl. Blonde, cheerleader, mean. So yeah, I think you can understand everything you need to know about her.

"BOO!"

I jumped, clutching my chest. Luna was laughing, and all I could do was roll my eyes. I really hate it when she does that.

"Seriously, Luna! What did I tell you about sneaking up on me like that?"

"Not to do it, but where's the fun in that? Anyway, that's not what I want to talk about. Why the hell are you stalking your ex's Instagram again? Thought you moved on from that crap."

"Wow, wow, I didn't realize I was being interrogated. And I wasn't stalking him. There's no reason for me to do that."

Lying wasn't my strongest suit. I mean, I wasn't really lying because I wasn't even stalking him. More like he popped up in my 'People you may know' and I clicked out of curiosity.

"Could it be that you're still madly in love with him?" Luna asked.

"Here we go again. I'm not 'still' madly in love with Kaiden. I am over him, so just drop it, will you?"

I was so not over him. There was just too much history between us in the past, and it definitely wasn't something to get over quickly. However, ending things was the best thing that we could do, and as much as it hurt, it was just the wrong time for us. Or it was the way he put it.

"Then I guess you wouldn't mind him being with someone else?"

My entire insides had dropped hearing that. But then I noticed the look on her face, which meant she was messing with me again. I didn't know why she was even bothering me. She didn't like us together because I spent way too much time with him and not enough with her, and I'd always get a damn earache anytime I told her I couldn't hang out with her because I was with Kaiden.

"Seriously, Hailey, it is time to MOVE ON! You guys broke up and you've not even batted an eye at anyone since then. Just get over it already."

"Really? Your best advice is to move on? How do you suppose I move on from the guy who was my first everything? I am not like you, Luna, who jumps into bed with anyone who has a penis. So please, don't stand there and say I am unreasonable."

She stood there with a scowl on her face. There weren't many times I stood up to her, but there were times when she needed to be reminded she was wrong. Like now. The last thing I'd do is take advice from someone who doesn't respect herself. Maybe I was overreacting, but when it came to my ex, Kaiden, there was no under-reacting. He was my very first love. I am someone who focuses on grades, but when I met him, something just changed. I remember it like it was yesterday.

We happened to be at the same party. I was only there because of Luna, and I stood in a corner sipping my water until it was time to go home. Then, just like some sappy romance movie, our eyes met, and my heart skipped a beat. I'm not sure if it was just my imagination or if it was happening for real, but when I saw him walking toward me, I hurriedly ran out. There was no way he was looking at me, I thought to myself. I found the gazebo in the back and realized it had a perfect view of the stars in the sky. To my surprise, he was there, too. I don't know how he knew I'd come here, but I wasn't complaining.
　"Sorry, I didn't realize anyone would be here."
　That's when I finally had the courage to talk to him, and he turned around, and I got a better look at him. I was shocked at how gorgeous he was. If there was such a thing as a perfect guy, he stood right in front of me.
　"You're fine. Plus, it was getting kind of lonely for all the two minutes I've been here." He joked.
　It made me giggle as I walked over next to him and we both stared at the same sky and the awkward silence took over. I apparently needed a script in order to talk to him. But thankfully, he broke the ice fast, which was a relief.
　"Needed some fresh air, huh?"

Him and I

You could almost hear the nervousness in his voice, but him saying that actually opened up an entire conversation. I know I was someone with no relationship experience, but Kaiden and I connected on a deeper level, and the conversation went from awkward to like we've known each other all our lives. That simple interaction went from talking to park dates, food dates, movie dates, or just days where he was there watching me while I studied. He used to say it was the best damn view. It wasn't hard to fall for Kaiden because he made it so easy, and I couldn't ask for a better first of everything. He took a part of me with him, so no, it wasn't easy and no, I don't want to get over him until I am ready.

But with something so amazing, you'd never realize what went wrong. It was written in the stars when he kissed me for the first time. This might sound cheesy, but I was floating on cloud nine when his lips connected with mine. I had never kissed a boy before, but kissing him came so naturally and that sudden fear turned into confidence. Like a perfect rhythm as our tongues danced together while his hand gripped my neck. And even though months had passed by, I would still get nervous anytime he was around. That's the type of effect he had on me. He knew what he was doing. Sometimes, it scared me that with him being so experienced and me being naive, he'd get bored. But he never made me feel that way. I remember what our first sleepover was like. I felt a little rebellious as he snuck into my room and he just held me. He wasn't pushing for anything but closeness. It felt like we completed each other, and I never wanted him to leave. Our relationship started to move faster and to me, it was everything a girl could ask for, especially the day when kissing turned into more than that.

A night that I'd never forget because it was the night that I thought I would lose him when he knew I was a virgin. I was lying on the couch as his hands rubbed my bare waist, slowly lifting my shirt over my head. I don't know what came over me at that moment, but I ended up sending him home. I don't know why I did that, though, because I honestly thought I was ready to go all the way, yet I just couldn't do it for some reason. Luckily, Kaiden wasn't mad about it and he kissed me goodnight and texted me when he got home. But even though he did that, I was still afraid that he might not want to speak to me again. However, we continued to see each other, and he never once acted differently or made me feel bad for saying "no" to him.

But then there was that night that changed everything, and the knot I had in my stomach the last time didn't exist anymore. We were at his place, sitting on each side of the couch, talking to each other. At some point, I stopped talking and just looked at him. And there was this moment, which I can't explain, but if I had to, it would be the realization that I was helplessly in love with this guy who had stolen my heart in such a short period. It was then I knew I had nothing to fear. It was my own insecurities holding me back. I wasn't even listening to what he was saying anymore when I threw myself at him and planted my lips on his. I made the first move, and that was something I never in a million years thought I would do. I knew he wouldn't object either since he had been waiting so patiently, and I was grateful for that. But I also knew that I needed to give him an explanation for what happened last time. I pulled back from the kiss and he just looked at me, confused. . .

"Kaiden, I need to tell you something. . . I am a virgin."

My heart was pounding like crazy and I had never been so nervous in my life as I was at that moment. I was waiting for his "What the fuck" reaction, but his face was the same. What was he even thinking right now? Why wasn't he saying anything? All these thoughts were making me freak out even more.

"You are?" He asked.

I just nodded and slowly lifted myself off of him, knowing that I ruined the entire mood. I didn't want him to look at me like I was fragile, but he deserved to know.

"Why haven't you told me?"

I bit on my bottom lip, trying to find an answer, but honestly, my reasoning seemed unfair.

"I don't know... I guess I thought you'd like me less."

"Like you less? Why would I do that? Sex isn't the only thing keeping me here and I never want to force you to do anything you don't want to. If you're not ready, that's okay. I am fine with just being near you."

Words of reassurance were all I needed. It felt so soon, but I was in love with him. There wasn't anything to worry about anymore. I was ready. In a moment, I pulled my top over my head and watched as his eyes scanned my entire body, but he seemed too afraid to touch it.

"I want you." I whispered.

And those words were all he needed before his hand grabbed the back of my neck and claimed my lips with his. The way his tongue found places I didn't know could feel pleasure! I got to experience what it was like to make love for the first time. It was a mix of pleasure and pain. The best part was *waking up with him still by my side. We had something special. I don't think I will ever find such a connection again. It's a shame to know that the cards weren't in our favor. When our paths just didn't cross anymore. And the stars stopped aligning. Kaiden and I both agreed that ending things was for the best. Sadly, since that day I've missed him a lot and now I was not so sure if it was the right choice.*

"Oh please! Just because he is your first doesn't mean he will be your last. Now stop with the moping and move on. It's time to find a second or a third or even a fourth."

"I am not you, so probably not."

The twitch in Luna's eyebrow had shown everything. I knew exactly what to do to get under her skin, and sometimes she really needed to be knocked from her pedestal.

"I'm going to let that slide because it's your birthday, but no worries. I am about to be the best wing woman to find your second tonight. While we party hardy."

At this point, I was sick of this conversation, so I just rolled my eyes as we headed inside for our next class. I didn't feel mentally or emotionally ready for someone else. The heartache Kaiden left me with is something that needed a long time to recover. I know it was supposed to be a mutual thing, but my heart wasn't prepared to admit that maybe he just stopped fighting for us. I couldn't give him what he needed and he couldn't give me the time, either. Maybe I should listen to Luna and attempt to move on from this pain now.

Chapter 3

School finally ended, and I headed to the front of school, where Luna was waiting for me like usual. I walked over and lightly tugged on her hair as payback for scaring me earlier.

"Argh! That hurt!" She yelled. "Seriously, there's something wrong with you, Hailey."

"Payback is a bitch."

She rolled her eyes at me, which was her only comeback. "Listen, don't forget to ask your dad, and let me know because it takes time to look this hot."

Before I could even answer her, she had walked away. That was her way of saying "The conversation is over". Now it was time to go home and ask my dad something I was pretty sure he'd say "no" to. I was his firstborn, and we had an amazing relationship, so I could understand why he'd be hesitant to say yes. But he also couldn't say "no" sometimes, especially when I gave him those puppy-dog eyes. I let out a little laugh before walking over to my shiny beamer and driving off. My mind started wandering to the conversation

Luna and I had. Kaiden-freaking-Scott. How could something so perfect be so disastrous? I remember this one time Kaiden and I went to the movies, and I was so nervous that I managed to drop hot cheese all over me. However, he walked out with no shirt on just so I wouldn't have to wear the cheese covered outfit. His loyalty was unquestionable, and it pained me to hear that some other girl was getting what I wanted. Someone who could give him the time that he deserved. I couldn't give him that sadly.

  Imagine being on the same path and suddenly you're on different pages of the book. It's crazy how things don't always go as planned and maybe if we had met at a different time, it would've worked out. I didn't realize I was zoned out before I slammed on my brakes, but it was too late when the front of my car had crashed into the back of a black Ferrari. You have got to be kidding me! There was no way my dad would say yes after this. I think it was the internal shock that set in and suddenly a knock on my window brought me out of my thoughts. Well, time to face the music. I reached for the door and got out of my car, but the sun was so bright that I had a hard time seeing.

  "I am so sorry. I wasn't paying attention."

  The man had his arms crossed and then I finally got a good look at him.

  "Yeah, it doesn't take a genius to realize that. But looks like you took most of the impact."

  He walked to the front of my car and started inspecting the damage and then looked at his. I reached into my car and pulled a piece of notebook paper and started writing my information for the stranger I just hit. I walked over and handed him the now folded-up piece of paper, but he didn't take it from me.

"Again, I am so sorry. It was not my intention."

My phone rang and I noticed it was Luna. This girl won't drop it for a minute. "Hey, I can't talk right now. I just rear-ended someone, so I don't think my dad will even approve of my birthday party when he finds out. I just turned 18, and I already screwed up."

"You're kidding me?" Luna exclaimed.

I couldn't stand hearing her bitching, so I hung up the phone and went back to the victim of my bad driving.

"Do you have someone that can pick you up?" He asked.

I was a little confused as to why he was asking me that, but I just nodded.

"I know someone who can fix your car up brand new in just a few days. Let me take care of this."

I was shocked by what he was saying. I mean, I was the one that hit him, not the other way around. "You don't have to do that. It was my fault."

The man had walked over to the side of my car and took my car key from the ring of my key chain and handed me the rest.

"Just call it a gift. Happy Birthday, Hailey. Now go and call someone, and the place will let you know when your car is ready to be picked up."

But it didn't strike me until he walked away. I knew that stranger, and he was no stranger.

"Hunter!" I called out.

He turned a tad bit and just smirked before proceeding to his car with his phone pressed to his ear. He was really not going to say anything. I pulled out my phone from my bag and called Brandon. He wasn't happy when I told him what happened and he had to come and pick me up as soon as possible. Maybe there were kind people out there and I wouldn't have to worry about Dad by narrating the entire accident to him. I could just say I left it at Luna's. I wasn't one to keep secrets or lie to my parents, but there were some things that were better left unsaid. We arrived at our house and when we walked in, Dad was furious, like he already knew something. How could he know, though? I think when I saw the smirk on my sister's face said it all.

"Why are you telling students that you'll be throwing your birthday party at my club, and I am the last one to know?"

My stomach just fell through my vagina. Why was she so dead set on ruining everything for me? I was going to ask him and technically it was Luna who spread the message prematurely.

"What!" I said, giving him a confused look.

"Answer me! Because you know damn well that's out of the question." My dad raised his voice.

I was a good person. I got good grades and never talked back. So why all of a sudden couldn't I make my own choices? Because my dad said so? But I guess that's what I get for being Daddy's little girl. Well, happy freaking birthday to me.

"It wasn't Hailey, it was me."

My thoughts were interrupted by my brother. He said he wasn't going and now he is backing me up? I think even Alyssa was surprised, because the steam that was coming out of her ears said it all.

"It slipped my mind, but I was going to ask you after school and the news already spread fast."

"You two want to throw a party at my club?"

Brandon and I looked at each other and then back at my annoyed father, who was now conflicted. He would never let me do anything if I didn't have someone to protect me like I am some fragile being.

"Come on, we are 18, Dad, and have never asked for much before." Brandon continued.

"I don't know if my club is the best place. You guys are still young."

It was about time that I busted out his weakness. There was nothing like the power his firstborn had when she really wanted something.

"Please, Daddy? I promise we will behave."

He stared at us for a while and finally, he broke down and let out a frustrated sigh. "Alright, fine! But don't let it get out of hand. I will have people watching you."

I ran to him and wrapped my arms around my father. And Alyssa just about had a fit. It still baffled me how much she tried to get under my skin. She never does this with Brandon, but with me, it's a fight for my father's affection.

"I can't believe you're going to let her go!"

She had stomped upstairs with such drama. Now, I had to call Luna and decide what outfit I was going to shine in tomorrow night. I wanted to let my hair down and let it loose. I made it this far without a smudge on my shoe that I deserved to have a little fun, and there was no one who was going to ruin that for me. My brother saved my ass and I couldn't be more grateful right now. On Saturday, I felt a nervous feeling in my stomach, but when it was time for the party, I took time to get ready early because it takes a while to look extra good. After my shower, I knew I needed to look my age, but also wanted to get a little messy tonight.

But what's a party without making a statement? I put on a little more makeup than usual and curled my long, deep-brown hair. Then I reached for that dress I've had for a while but never wore, but knew I would eventually. I slipped the gold dress until it was firmly wrapped around my body. The dress had a slit on the side and a V-neck that exposed my breast but also pushed them tightly together. I loved how it snatched my waist and no day was more important for a dress like this than the day of being a legal adult. After hours of getting ready, I walked downstairs to where I was met with my brother. He sort of looked annoyed that he was going instead of hanging out with his girlfriend alone. It was our birthday, though, so I think he owed me this day. We got into his car to begin our drive to my dad's club. He had closed it down for just my friends and me.

"Thank you for this, Brandon. I know you'd rather be with Diora. But it means a lot that you have my back."

My brother and I were close, but not up each other's ass close. I think with us being twins, it was just a little easier to understand each other. Sometimes we feel what the other feels, and we say exactly what the other is thinking.

"I can hang out with her alone later. She doesn't mind hanging out for a bit. Plus, it might be fun celebrating our birthday. But I want you to be honest with me about something, Hailey."

"Okay. Honest about what?"

"Did you really want to have this party or was it Luna pressuring you? I've known you long enough to know that the party scene isn't really you."

I let out an exhale and just thought of being honest with him or just staying in denial. I think a part of me wanted me to want this, but deep down, doing something so big wasn't what I wanted. I wasn't one to complain either, so I allowed for it to happen and who knows? Maybe I might have fun.

"She means well, but her way of fun is different from mine. When she gets pushy and her voice starts screeching, I just say yes so, I don't have to hear it anymore."

"Yeah, I know, but you don't always have to do what she says. And honestly, who the fuck cares what she wants?"

"I don't always do what she wants, okay? I have a brain of my own."

I tried to argue, but it only led to Brandon rolling his eyes at me.

"You do. All the time. You're not a confrontational person, so you just go with the flow."

My brother was right. Sometimes it was just so hard to say no to Luna because she was someone who would get snarky over the smallest thing. Sometimes when I'm not in the mood to hang out with her, I have to come up with an excuse to get out of it. Otherwise, she would get offended and make me feel guilty. However, she isn't always like this. I think she's just used to us being together nonstop since the start of middle school, and therefore she acts this way.

We had finally pulled up to the club and now my anxiety had set in and my palms started sweating. We walked to the door and suddenly, when it opened, the uneasy feeling I had just a few seconds ago had disappeared.

"HAPPY BIRTHDAY!"

Everyone had said in unison, which left me shocked while screaming. I looked at Luna and realized she did all this.

Melia A

This is why she is my best friend. Even when she is pushy, she still does these small things that make me happy to have her as a friend. Somehow, us being two different people went well together, and it worked.

Chapter 4

Zane walked over and gave me a hug. Luna was already at my side, but I know their amount of bickering is their type of flirting, but she would never admit it.

"You look beautiful, Hales."

"Thank you." I replied.

I withdrew from his hug and watched as Luna rolled her eyes at him.

"Don't worry, Luna. You look almost as good as Hailey. Sorry, you tried so hard, though."

I took a step back and just waited until their flirting was ending. I was waiting for her to stop being so stubborn and admit she liked him. But she had an issue with the fact that he was one of the good guys and not a bad boy. She likes assholes. Just like Hunter, who she can't seem to get over after their one night on the side of the club, but there is nothing I can do to change her mind.

"I'd rather show you something else." I finally tuned in to what they were saying and I listened in at the wrong time because Zane had already walked away, but not before Luna gave her infamous grunt.

"He is so annoying!" She yelled.

"Yeah, I'm pretty sure he's into you."

Her face showed she was disgusted, but I know deep down she felt the exact same way. But he wasn't a bad boy, like I said. We walked toward the bar to get water, well for me. Luna divulged herself in some tequila, knowing damn well it makes her clothes fall out.

"Seriously, Hales, it's your birthday! Have a little fun."

She tried to hand me a shot, but I waved it off. I can have fun without my mind getting all groggy. I took a sip from my water, but when she turned around, it dropped.

"Hailey, what the fuck is Kaiden doing here!"

I stopped for a moment and looked in the direction she was looking, and suddenly, I felt high. It didn't seem real because I hadn't seen him in months. I know I had hoped many times that he would show up randomly and it was some kind of fairytale, but I wasn't prepared for this. I didn't expect to see Kaiden at my birthday party. I was in shock, and so many questions were running through my mind. One of them was, what the hell is he doing here? He walked in as if he owned the place, and everyone was staring at him. Some of them were even drooling. But who could blame them? Just looking at him was proof enough. He was six-foot-tall, with tanned skin that perfectly matched his chocolate brown messy hair.

Sometimes he could be a little intimidating, especially when he looks at you with those eyes... Gray as the sea. He would look at you so intensively and deeply that it felt like he was staring into your soul.

"Oh my God, he brought Hunter too!" Luna yelled.

Then it made perfect sense how he knew I was here. Hunter must have overheard me talking to Luna the other day, and then he probably told Kaiden about it.

"I think I'm having a panic attack."

I felt my chest viciously going up and down, all while trying to catch my breath. I wasn't sure if I wanted him here, to begin with, but there he was.

"Jesus, Hailey! Stop being so dramatic."

Maybe I was being dramatic, but it was Kaiden Scott. My first and only love. I had every right to be dramatic. His eyes were now looking at me, and my legs started moving on their own. The moment I got a whiff of his cologne, it set me back at how many times I had inhaled it before, and it was one of my favorite scents. But we aren't together now, so I can't show him how nervous he still makes me feel.

"What are you doing here?" I asked.

But there was no hiding the stutter in my voice. He eyed me from head to toe a little longer before he finally spoke.

"Well. Hello to you too, Hales. It's nice to see you again."

"Just answer the question, will you?"

"I forgot what the question was. Ask that again, it's so loud in here."

This guy was really acting like he couldn't hear me. The music was loud but not loud enough to where he couldn't hear me.

"Seriously, Kaiden? You're wasting my time."

He started smirking before slowly walking backward.

"If you want to talk to me, I suggest we go somewhere quieter."

He winked at me and continued toward the back rooms that were unoccupied. I never even knew stripper poles were back there.

"Really? A stripper pole? Does this mean you're going to strip for me? Or since it's your birthday, maybe you want me to strip for you?"

"No one is stripping. Now please just explain why you're here?"

He rolled his eyes, almost disappointed, but that's just the type of guy he was. Never stopped flirting with me, even when we were dating. However, I couldn't think this way, not now.

"Well, I saw Luna's viral post about your birthday party, and also your damaged car from hitting Hunter, so I wanted to come and wish you a happy birthday in person instead of sending you a text message."

"You wanted to text me?" I blurted.

Here I just melted into his hands once again. He looked at me the way he used to and I hated him for it. It would be so much easier if he was mean to me because I can't forget him.

"I did, but I forgot to bring you a present."

"It's fine. I don't need any presents."

He just stared at me one more time before he made his way over to me and suddenly, he was only inches apart. All that confidence I had just a second ago vanished.

"What do you need then, Hales?"

I had to be dreaming. He was so close, but we weren't together, so there had to be some kind of boundary. So, I took a step back to put some distance between us, hopefully trying to get the point across. To my surprise, he took a step forward with once again being close to me.

"Aren't you hot in that jacket?" He whispered.

"No, I—"

But before I could finish my sentence, he slid it off my arms, and it made a thud when it hit the ground. My heart raced at his touch. I've been longing for him when he was no longer touching me and I wish he didn't stop. I finally had the nerve to look up and, just like before, there was this connection between us that was undeniable.

"Why are you looking at me like that?"

"Like what?" He asked back.

Suddenly, I felt naked and uncomfortable. As much as I liked where this was going, there was just so much that happened to allow it to go any further, but I can't say I didn't enjoy him being here. I wrapped my arms around my chest, trying to shield myself from I don't know what, but the dress I had on just wasn't enough.

"You don't have to cover up for me, babe. I've already seen and touched every inch of your body." He said, smirking at me.

***

Luna

I can't believe she went with him after everything he had done. I never liked Kaiden. He was just the type of guy who thinks he can flash his award-winning smile and get whatever he wants. Not to mention how naive Hailey can be sometimes. I should've stopped her, but I basically encouraged her to go with him. I wandered around the club searching for her, but knowing her, she must have been probably floating on fucking rainbows now that he's back. I weaved in and out of the crowd and even the bathrooms. I tried to call her a few times, but her phone just rang and went to voicemail each time.

"Who are you looking for?"

My body suddenly froze. I knew that voice anywhere. I turned around to see that stoic expression of Hunter's. Just the sight of him made my blood boil. I hated him, especially after he treated me so horribly. He was just your typical fuck-boy. But there was no denying that he was the sexiest man I've had the chance of feeling inside me.

"Long time no see, Luna. Miss me?"

He had that stupid but delicious smirk that I liked so much, and if I wasn't trying to save Hailey from Kaiden, then maybe just maybe. . .

"No, as a matter of fact, I haven't missed you at all. Not even a single thought. You must not be memorable enough."

He laughed out loud.

"Same, talk about a waste of a nice night."

He reached into his pocket, grabbed a cigarette, and lit it. Could this guy get any sexier with how he defies the law?

"Whatever. Why are you and Kaiden here? You guys weren't even invited."

"Luna, Luna, Luna . . . Let me tell you something. I'm Hunter Lockwood. I don't need invitations. I can go anywhere and leave as I please. There is no one who is going to tell me differently. Capiche?"

He sucked on the cigarette some more right before he flicked it on the ground and stomped on it. Why was he so fucking hot yet so dangerous all in one? He and I could have been perfect for each other. Like a ride-or-die situation. But being the asshole he is, he had to ruin everything. I finally snapped out of my lustful thoughts, and he was still standing there.

"Just tell me where Hailey and Kaiden went."

If I were to stay here with him any longer, I don't think I could resist throwing myself at him because it seemed like the tequila was starting to get the better of me.

"How the fuck should I know where they went? Do I look like their keeper? They're probably fucking somewhere for all I care."

I didn't want to think that because she shouldn't get back with the loser who couldn't handle it when things got tough. I needed to find her quickly.

***

Hailey

I could smell the mint in Kaiden's breath, and the way his cologne engulfed me sent me back to when he was on top of me.

"So. . ."

I snapped out of my thoughts when my phone vibrated. I looked at the screen and noticed that it was someone who would never call me.

"Zane?" I whispered.

But apparently, it was already too loud for Kaiden to hear me say it.

"Who's Zane?"

The hint of jealousy when he said it made me want not to answer him. I don't know why I wanted to get under his skin, but it seemed like a fun idea. I rolled my eyes at him before answering the call.

"Hey, what's up?"

I listened for a bit and he told me there was a situation. But as soon as he told me what kind of situation it was, my blood began to boil. I swear my sister could never let me have any fun. She was dead set on killing me from stress.

"Are you fucking kidding me? What is she even doing here?"

When I heard Alyssa was in trouble, I wished I didn't have to be the responsible one here. She was so damn immature it drove me insane. I hung up the phone and let out a frustrated sigh. "My annoying sister is here when she's not supposed to be, and she's in some kind of trouble. I have to go."

I quickly made my way back to the dance floor and saw exactly what was happening. There was this guy who was standing way too damn close. Before I could do anything, Kaiden had already walked that way and he was more than pissed at this.

Chapter 5

"Kaiden, what are you doing?" I yelled.

The guy tried to get closer to my sister, but before he could put his hands on her, Kaiden gripped his arms, and now they were inches apart. I wish I wasn't so frustrated at him because it was hot the way he was a protector. I couldn't quite hear what was going on, but the guy's demeanor had changed completely. I walked a bit closer so that I could hear what they were saying.

"I was just joking with her, man, chill."

But that seemed to piss Kaiden off. I wasn't going to stand for it when he started to walk away. My sister may be annoying, but she was still my sister. I stood in front of him before he was leaving to stare him down.

"She's a fucking child, you pervert! When someone says no, then leave it the hell alone. What don't you understand?"

I grabbed a drink from someone who walked by and poured it down his shirt. He jumped from the freezing ice and now he was angry. But before he could do anything worse,

Kaiden had put space between him and I. When the pervert walked away our attention went back to Alyssa.

"Are you okay?" Kaiden asked her.

"Yeah, I'm okay."

This bitch was trifling as she started thanking him and giving him those flirtatious eyes. I could never have anything for myself. What I had, she wanted. My blood started boiling again, and I walked over and snatched her arm while yelling at her, but didn't make it that far.

"HAILEY?"

I turned around to see my dad standing there, completely furious. Great! The moment he puts his trust in me is when he shows up. My palms started to become clammy just by staring at him.

"I got a call from one of my employees, and he told me Alyssa is here. Where is she?"

In most cases, I'd probably avoid this, but seeing the eyes she gave Kaiden made my stomach turn. I was lenient about most things, but one thing I won't stand for is her thinking she has a chance with him. She was a damn kid, for Christ's sake. I moved to the side so he could get a better view, and once he saw her, the steam was coming out of his eyes.

"What the hell is she wearing? Also, why is she with your ex? Wait, why is Kaiden here?"

"He helped her get out of trouble." I said, rolling my eyes.

My dad had stormed past me and made his way over to them. I slowly walked closer to watch this whole mess unfold. The moment Kaiden noticed my dad, you could see how uncomfortable he got. My father was a calm man, but he looked intimidating. However, when he gets mad, you see an entirely different side of him, as it's rare to see him so riled up.

"I thought your dad wasn't coming. God, he's such a DILF!"

I looked beside me and saw Luna's horny ass basically eye fucking my dad. She didn't have any type of filter and that's where I draw the line, but she always crosses it.

"Luna, can you please stop!"

"What? He's hot. If he weren't married to your mom, I would definitely fu—"

I yanked on her hair, stopping her from finishing that sentence. She let out a low "Owww". I turned my attention back to my father, who was giving Alyssa the death stare. Kaiden was now by my side, watching them with me. She was absolutely terrified. My dad had grabbed onto her back and forced her out of the club. Damn, that was a different type of walk of shame.

"Sorry. Hailey, but I need to go now." Kaiden informed.

"You're leaving already?" I said in a surprised tone.

I felt a tug on my heart because we didn't really have much of a chance to talk because my sister had to kill that mood.

"Then go, because no one cares."

I turned to Luna and glared at her while Kaiden let out a hoarse laugh. I honestly didn't know what her big deal was. She literally acted like Kaiden broke up with her and not me.

"What? No one cares if he leaves. So just let the fuck-boy go." Luna continued.

My eyes met the back of my head. She was fine two seconds ago and now, all of a sudden, she was hurt and dismissive.

"Obviously you don't care, so I guess that makes you no one." Kaiden replied. "No one that matters to me, anyway."

I covered my mouth, trying to keep the laugh from coming out. He was always a smart ass with his answers. Usually, I'd say something, but she was wrong in the way she treated him. Everything always had to be a fight with her. But I guess that's what happens when you put the nice girl and the mean girl together.

"Well, you kinda started it, so. . . Don't get mad now."

I tried to walk away, but she wouldn't let it go as usual. "Excuse me?"

I exhaled and turned around to face her. Why did everything have to be a fight? Why was it that she wanted to keep poking the bear and was surprised when it bit back?

"What? You can't expect him to be nice to you when you're being rude to him."

"I wasn't being rude. I was simply telling the truth."

I just rolled my eyes at her and walked away. This was a battle I wouldn't win, so why even waste my breath on her? She yelled after me, but I completely ignored her. I was so ready to leave at this point because the entire night was already ruined. When I got outside, I was surprised to see Hunter there.

"Hunter!"

Hunter Lockwood. I've mentioned him a few times, but who really was he? To be honest, I wasn't too sure myself. He's quite a mysterious person. He looked at me with his blazing hazel eyes that sent shivers down my spine. I couldn't help but check him out from head to toe. He looked dangerous.

He had multiple earrings in his left ear and a piercing in his bottom lip. His dark hair was perfectly done in a tapered way. Strong muscles tightened against the black shirt he was wearing, showing off his chestnut skin covered in tattoos.

I've only shared a few brief words with him. I don't know if it's because he's not much of a talker and therefore, we've never had anything to talk about. He and Kaiden are very close friends, almost like brothers. They've known each other since they were kids. He's pretty cocky and arrogant. However, he can be nice too. Well, sometimes. I guess it all depends on what mood he's in. He can also be very intimidating, and I know for a fact that many people are scared of him. I've heard some rumors that he's part of a gang, but Kaiden assured me those were only rumors and nothing more. So, I never brought it up again and kind of forgot about it. Now he was standing in front of me, and I felt so awkward in my own shoes.

"Let me guess. You're looking for Kaiden, am I right?"

I stood there with my arms crossed around my chest, just staring at him. I could now add a few sentences to the handful of words he's said.

"Unfortunately, he has already left."

"Do you perhaps know why he was in such a hurry?" I asked.

Hunter had reached into his pocket and pulled out a pack of cigarettes. He slowly pulled one out and lit it, leaving a cloud of smoke in the air. I watched as he inhaled and exhaled before he finally spoke.

"I mean, I could, but then I'd have to kill you."

My heart was about to beat out of my chest with the way he sounded so sinister. I gulped hard, and I was pretty sure he heard it. Going back to the party felt no better.

"Relax, princess. I'm just fucking with you. But you should've seen your face. It was priceless." He chuckled.

"Yeah, well, you have a weird sense of humor then."

He finished the rest of the cig before he flicked it past me. I think deep down, he knew he intimidated people, and it seemed like it brought him some kind of joy whenever that happened.

"Anyway, Kaiden had to go and take care of something. That's pretty much all I can tell you. Have a nice evening, Hailey."

There was a hint of arrogance in his voice while he dragged out the last syllable of my name. I watched as he walked away and then stopped in his tracks.

"Oh, and happy birthday again. Try to stay away from operating vehicles."

He gave me that sadistic smile before continuing his walk until he was non-existent from my view. Apparently, he talks more than I thought. I made my way back to the club when I stopped and watched as Luna threw herself at Zane. I knew she had a thing for him and maybe it was the liquor that finally gave her the courage to make a move on him. I went in a different direction so that I wouldn't ruin their little moment.

After a few more hours, I finally got home and my feet were literally balloons from these uncomfortable high heels that I walked in on different types of grounds the whole night. When I got to my room, I saw a dark shadow, and I nearly peed my pants. But once I turned on the light, it was no one but my sister.

"You scared me! What the hell are you doing in my room, Alyssa?" I asked.

She looked at me with no emotions whatsoever. Usually, she'd look at me with that stare that's full of hate and jealousy, but this time it was different. It was just a blank stare.

"Nothing, I was just returning your clothes." She answered.

"About that. Who even gave you permission to wear my clothes? Mom and Dad would never approve of it, and neither would I!"

Now her entire demeanor switched.

"I did." She snapped back.

"Excuse me? I don't want you touching my clothes ever again, or anything of mine, for that matter. Do I make myself clear?"

She rolled her eyes at me, telling me to calm down, but I was anything but calm.

"By the way, are you and Kaiden back together?"

"I don't think that's any of your business. Why are you even asking me this?"

The right side of her mouth went up like she was smirking at me. She was weird sometimes. But I didn't trust her, especially not after the way she had acted with Kaiden earlier.

"Just asking. Have a good night."

I watched as she walked away, but then my mind drifted to Kaiden. We never got to finish what we were talking about. I still had so many questions to ask him, like why was he really there in the first place? Because I didn't believe for a second that he only came to wish me "happy birthday". I debated texting him for a few minutes before I finally found the courage to do so.

Hailey: Hi, Kaiden.

Hailey: I just wanted to say thank you. I never had the chance to do it at the club since you were in a rush to leave. Anyway, goodnight.

I threw my phone on the bed, realizing I actually just texted him, and every doubt had entered my mind like this was a stupid idea. I know I was just trying to see him again because why wouldn't I? I hadn't gotten over him and probably never would. I quickly changed my clothes and made myself comfortable in bed. All the overthinking made me exhausted to where I passed out.

When I woke up, I was still feeling anxious because he had read my message but never responded. I mean, we weren't together, so he didn't owe me anything, right? But it didn't help my anxiety or the fact that last night felt like a horrible dream. Seeing Kaiden was both terrible, but amazing at the same time. When we broke up, it felt like it was the end. And when I didn't see him after that, I knew it was beyond over. Yet last night he was there. . . In front of me. Like nothing had ever changed. My mind was fogged, and I knew I needed to shake the feeling off. I put on my purple sports bra and some black shorts before I went downstairs and back to reality. Even though he was still on my mind.

Chapter 6

I went downstairs and was greeted by my mom, who was cooking already. I was lucky that I came out with her genes that allowed me to be tall and eat whatever I want without gaining a pound, but a run never hurts anyone.

"Hey, Mom, I am going out for a run."

"Okay, but not for long. Dinner will be ready soon."

I grabbed my headphones and began to set it up when I noticed Alyssa walking in with a donut in her hand. Her eyes just burned a hole in the side of my cheek and I knew right then and there she was about to say something stupid.

"Be careful. You don't want to get lost in the woods and perhaps come up missing." She said before taking a bite of her donut.

"You would like that, wouldn't you?"

We both started going back and forth, and it took my mom a moment to raise her voice enough to get our attention. She is a kid and I don't understand why I allow her to get under my skin the way that she does.

"Okay, enough, you two! Can't you two be a little nicer to each other?"

But I think it would honestly kill her to be any type of nice to me. I mean, she stole my clothes, which means she likes my style, but she'd never admit it.

"I am nice." She shrugged.

I felt like my eyes were going to get stuck in the back of my head with how hard I rolled them. I mean, we all know she is some bitter teenager. I didn't want to entertain this anymore, so I walked away. I put my headphones on and as soon as this light cold weather hit my skin, I darted toward the sidewalk. I got lost in my music, just needing some type of escape. Between make up and break up songs, nothing mattered at this moment. If I allowed my thoughts to take over, I'd fall into a dark place. Therefore, I needed to get out and clear my mind. I wasn't able to sleep during the night after my encounter with Kaiden last night. The magical moment in the room before Zane called felt like how it was back then. God! How I've missed those days! In a few weeks, it will almost be four months since we broke up, yet it felt like it happened yesterday. As I was jogging, suddenly someone came rushing from my right and before I knew it, I was face planting the ground. Pain ran through my body as I rubbed my arms and face from the impact. I looked up and once again, my eyes were deceiving me. What the fuck was Kaiden doing here in the middle of nowhere? And now that I looked around, I thought to myself, where was I even?

"Kaiden?"

I spoke in a shocked tone while he just stood there. Calm as the night, just looking me up and down like I had some explaining to do. He watched as I rubbed my now scratched-up elbow and guilt washed over his face. The confident guy I saw last night just melted in front of me.

"Are you okay?" He questioned.

I just nodded my head because I was still shocked as to what he was doing here.

"What are you doing out here?"

My eyebrow raised at him like he is really asking me that? I rolled my eyes at him before taking my jacket off and noticing the hole that was now in it, not maintaining eye contact.

"That's actually none of your business."

I walked past him, but he grabbed my arm. I was frustrated that he still hadn't told me where he went last night, why he was back, and why he didn't even respond to my text?

"Feisty, aren't we?"

His eyes searched every inch of my body like he was ready to devour it. Irritation was spiking again. I hated not knowing, and this suspense was driving me insane.

"Judging by your clothes, I'm pretty sure you were out on a run."

Smart fucking ass, that man was.

"Trying to stay fit, huh?"

"Yep. But it's not the reason why I was out running. Now if you don't mind, I want to continue my run without any ex-boyfriends slamming into me."

I walked past him and he just started walking next to me. I should've run, but a part of me was enjoying the moment.

"Well, next time you wanna go for a run, do me a favor and do it where there are people around. Now let me walk you home."

Even though I wanted that more than anything, there had to be some boundaries, and there were still a lot of unanswered questions. I wasn't really comfortable allowing him in when he was part of the reason for my heart breaking into a dozen pieces. Kaiden Scott was so much more than the man I loved, but he took my first everything and all those plans and promises he made were just empty words. I know we both agreed to this, but that didn't mean that I couldn't feel betrayed. He didn't fight for me, for us, so I just let him go. Like we were reading the same book but were on completely different pages. Maybe it was probably for what's best, but now a part of me was protecting myself from that type of heartbreak again. Even when the other part of me wanted to reach over and plant my lips on his. This break has allowed me to learn boundaries and know when sometimes I can't act on impulses, but man, it was so hard.

"Thanks, but I can walk by myself."

I cut past him, but he was relentless.

"I know you can, but I'd rather walk you home, just in case."

"Thanks, Kaiden, but my house is nearby. I'll be home in no time."

I think he was disappointed judging by the look on his face, but I looked past it. I couldn't get sucked in the way I used to when I melted in his arms.

"I'll text you when I get home, so don't worry."

He gave me a smirk and this time he didn't stop me from walking by. However, I felt his stare until I was far from his sight. I decided to walk instead of running now to soak up the night sky. Walks were more calming, and I needed it after the way my heart just skipped a few beats. I cut through the park when I halted in my tracks. This night just got even weirder. I mean, first Kaiden and now Hunter?

"Hailey? What the hell are you doing here? Especially this late?" He questioned once he spotted me. His concerned tone went from worried to cold again.

"Nothing, I was just on my way home."

His face finally softened again and his stare had me questioning things. He wasn't a guy of many words, but he was sure a mystery. However, it started to get a bit uncomfortable with the way he was staring and not speaking. Like what was going through his mind? Especially about me, what was he thinking? I opened my mouth to kill the silence before he beat me to it.

"Well, what are you waiting for? Keep walking."

He spit those words out and now my sudden interest in his thoughts just disappeared.

"Excuse me? That's a bit rude, don't you think?"

His eyes rolled, and he went to being rude again! I couldn't understand why he treated me as if I ever did him wrong, except for hitting his car, but that didn't count as a reason since it happened recently.

"You can't be here right now, alright?" He finally spoke.

I saw as his finger tapped on his crossed arm like me being there made him anxious.

"Why not?" I asked.

"For fuck's sake, Hailey! Don't you have some homework to do or something?"

I could tell that me being there was actually pissing him off for some odd reason. Both Kaiden and he were acting strange in just some random places at random times. Was this some odd version of hide and seek, or what?

"Yes, but I want to take a quick break before I go home. I'm a little tired after my jog."

"Look, you can't take a break here. I'm meeting some people in a few minutes, so you can't be here, alright!"

I just stared at him and suspicion grew inside me. My mind went to those rumors, and I couldn't help but wonder if they were actually true after all. However, I didn't want to be there to find out either. My life already had enough drama and the last thing I needed was to get involved in a dangerous situation.

"Fine. I'll leave."

I went to pass him, but his words stopped me in my tracks when he called my name.

"You shouldn't be jogging by yourself at night. There are people out there who would have no problem hurting a girl like you."

His words sent chills down my spine. Both he and Kaiden were just overly worried, which was strange. I didn't reply. Instead, I just started jogging and disappeared from there as fast as I could. When I got back to the house, my mom was waiting in the living room, basically freaking out.

"I was about to call the cops! You said you were going to be here in an hour." She yelled.

"Sorry, Mom, I bumped into Kaiden on my way home and lost track of time."

"Oh, you did? I thought your dad was lying when he said he was at your birthday party last night. Are you two back together, or what's going on?"

Of course, she would assume that.

"No, Mom, we're not back together. He just came by to wish me a happy birthday, that's all."

"Aww, that's sweet of him. Seems like he still cares about you. Why did you two break up again?"

I was so not wanting to have this conversation, knowing I just had the last twenty-four hours of overthinking everything that happened between us.

"Because of school. I was too busy with homework and things just didn't work out. And that pretty much drove us apart."

My mind drifted to that night. . .

"You're late. Again."

I looked at Kaiden and saw annoyance on his face. He knows things haven't been easy since I took my SATS and I have been doing so much to make sure I had straight As. He knew that from the beginning how important this was to me and now he is bitter about me working so hard? Like I am supposed to drop everything and get distracted so he doesn't feel alone? Was he really that selfish?

"I know, I'm sorry. But I had to finish some homework before I could come here. I really need those good grades to get into the college I want to attend. You know it's important to me."

He was looking at me with such distaste, and it wasn't even that serious.

"It seems like you are always too busy for me, and well, maybe you should just focus on school instead. So that I don't have to hear how sorry you are, or being stood up half the time."

I felt like my heart was crying out, telling him he was wrong, but he was right. I have been doing that. He should understand me, though. How come he isn't supporting me now?

"What do you mean by that?"

I tried to stop my voice from cracking, but it always seemed to find its way out. He let out a sigh as he walked over to me with his hands in his front pocket until we were inches apart.

"You're a smart girl, Hales. I think you know what I mean by that."

He's right, I do. I could sense it since I got here and now, with his patronizing voice, I knew exactly what he meant by it.

"So, you want to break up?"

"No, I don't want to. But it's for the best. Don't you think?"

I shook my head at it because to me it wasn't for the best, but I wasn't going to allow him to see me this way. If he wanted to end things, he could have his way. Why would I fight if he stopped fighting?

"We barely see each other lately. What kind of relationship is even that?"

I tried to wipe the tear before it escaped my eye.

"Look, I know school is very important to you, and this is why I think it's for the best if we end things. Because I don't want to be that person who distracts you, and you end up not getting the grades you want."

I went with what I know. Shutting down and agreeing. Making it seem like we both wanted this. I was in love with him and he walked away when things got hard. Maybe I was the issue, but I know I would've fought for us if the roles were reversed. I guess it's true what they say. Sometimes you will fight harder than others would do for you and this proved.

"Yeah, you're right."

I wiped my face, that was soaked in tears, and took one last look at him before turning around. I wanted to look back. I wanted him to stop me, but I knew he wouldn't. And if I looked, he wouldn't even be looking back.

"Yeah, I remember. I'm sorry." My Mom interrupted.

"Yeah, me too."

I decided a shower was well needed and the last thing I wanted to do was talk about my breakup with Kaiden for another second. I let the water cascade down my body. Boiling hot wasn't enough to not think about him. Him showing up, reminded me of everything. This exact shower where he had me slammed against the wall with his teeth on my neck as the friction from the water on our bodies made it all more pleasurable. He knew exactly what to touch. . . What angle before I was. . .

"Hey, are you done? Dinner is getting cold."

I came to reality at the sound of my sister's voice and then I realized what just happened as I looked down and saw the mess on my hands.

"Yeah, I'll be right down!" I shouted.

I finished cleaning up and saw that my sister was still in my room.

"Get out!" I demanded.

But she stood there with her arms crossed and that stupid smile on her face like she was better than everyone.

"Just making sure you come down."

She turned around, but then faced me again.

"Where were you, by the way? You disappeared." She asked.

"I ran into Kaiden on the way home, so I lost track of time."

She still stood there, which was strange. She seemed like she was up to something, but I couldn't quite put my finger on what it could be. After dinner, I went to bed and just wanted to forget this entire day. It seemed like I wasn't the only one acting like I did something they regret. When I got to school the next day, Luna was yelling at Zane and she blew a fuse. I didn't interrupt them. She was probably going to tell me about it later anyway. We finally arrived in class and Luna's eyes were filled with anger.

"Alright, tell me what's wrong? What was that all about in the halls with Zane?"

I was more curious than anything. When she gets all riled up, it makes me kind of laugh because it's usually over the silliest things.

"Zane! He's a jerk! I HATE HIM!" She yelled.

"Zane? He is the sweetest, though. What did he do now?"

"That jerk is acting like he doesn't remember our kiss."

Oh, hold the fuck up! They kissed? I was shocked because that boy had been in love with her for as long as I could remember, but she was all about dating the popular guy. Hell, when I dated Kaiden she was pissed that I was getting attention for dating the college boy, and everyone in school thought I was cool because of him. I didn't care about any of that, though.

"You guys kissed?"

She placed her hand over my mouth, telling me to shut up.

"Sorry, it just slipped out of my mouth. But now I need all the details! Who? What? When? Where? Why? How?!"

For the rest of the class period, we talked about it, but she didn't want to spill any details other than the basic stuff. She was really ashamed. She sure knew how to pick them. I mean, she was the idiot who hooked up with Hunter after I told her not to do it. She falls for a guy so fast, and ends up being fucked in some nasty alley, and he just walking off without even giving her a ride home. I still hear about that until this day.

But we all have our own issues. She was afraid of being forgotten. I was afraid of being alone. . . Kaiden, Hunter. Well, their issues ran deeper than I knew.

Chapter 7

Kaiden

Why do I do this? What kind of person spends his time scraping his mother off the ground because she drank herself to oblivion? Over the same thing each time. I've sacrificed so much, but at the end of the day, she is my mother. She found out my dad had a new girlfriend, and she just hasn't managed it even close to well enough.

I quickly helped her to bed and confronted her about the situation, and I was already late, but this was something I have been dealing with since my split with Hailey. There were a lot of things I never told her. It wasn't because I didn't trust her, but I just couldn't tell her. She had a good heart, and she was too curious to not want to fix things. But broken things never heal correctly. As soon as my mom had fallen asleep. I quickly grabbed my keys and headed out to meet Hunter.

"Where the fuck have you been, man? I've been waiting for twenty fucking minutes now."

I rolled my eyes, as he can be just a little too much sometimes. He was my best friend, and I was the only one he'd ever allowed to talk to him in any type of way.

"Twenty minutes isn't even long. Get your thong out your ass."

I quickly put my jacket on as he scowled at me. I was surprised how he wasn't wrinkled by now for how much he frowns in a day.

"When it comes to business, it is!"

I couldn't help but laugh when he gets worked up this way.

"Okay, chill. I had to take care of something." I responded.

"Take care of what?"

I let out the breath I was holding in. Only he knew me more than anyone. It was a type of friendship you can talk about anything with. However, Hunter was more of a brick wall with things like this.

"Just my mom. She found out about my dad's new girlfriend. I knew she would act this way, which is why I didn't tell her anything, to begin with."

I reached into my pocket and took out my cigarette box before lighting one up to relieve the stress. Hunter reached over and took one from the pack as well to unwind with me.

"Well, I can't say I feel sorry for her. Apparently, since I'm an emotionless asshole. But I must admit that your dad is a lucky bastard to have that kind of girlfriend at his age."

I rolled my eyes again.

"Don't roll your eyes at me. She's hot, and you know it."

"Yeah, and she's a gold digger. If my dad didn't have any money, she wouldn't even look his way."

I took another drag from my cig.

"How old is she again?" He asked.

"25 or some shit like that."

Hunter took a drag and thought for a second before letting out a laugh.

"Yep, she's definitely a gold digger then. Have you met her yet?"

I shook my head as I took the last drag before throwing the cigarette to the ground and stomping on it.

"Maybe they will invite you for dinner and I will be your date. Once your dad looks away, she will be on my dick before you know it. The ladies love me." He joked.

I think the annoyed look on my face made him want to keep pressing. Nosy motherfucker, he was.

"Why not? If it's not me, then who would you take? Unless you're back to sulking and you'd rather go alone." He hit my shoulder jokingly.

"Maybe I will take Hailey. She's a lot prettier than you. Plus, she won't try to fuck my dad's girlfriend."

We both started laughing at that. He topped off his cig before flicking it somewhere and straightened his jacket.

"Oh right. You're still in love with her, aren't you?"

When I didn't answer, he started laughing again and teasing me about it.

"Well, I can't blame you, man. She's something else. A little boring and too good for her own good, but she got a nice ass on her."

I looked at him, pissed. He knew better than to talk about her like that. Not like he cared, though. He always said what he wanted and didn't care if it was too far. If someone drew a visible line, Hunter would purposely step over and wait for the repercussions.

"Watch your mouth." That came out angrier than I meant for it to sound.

***

Hailey

"I'm kinda in the mood to throw a party this Friday."

I was reaching inside my locker to get changed when Luna and her random thoughts came out. She was standing in just her towel with that prissy look on her face.

"Whatever you want, Luna. I will be home enjoying the comfort of my own house."

I turned around with my clothes in my hands, looking at her and thought, here we go. I clearly said something she didn't agree with.

"The hell you are!" She retorted.

"Why not?"

"Because what kind of boring party would that be? You have to come!"

She grabbed onto my hand, just pleading for me to come. I sighed as I rolled my eyes at her.

"Stop being so damn boring, Hailey."

Seriously? She always did this when I didn't want to do what she wanted to. Called me boring. We get along, but we are two different people. Partying was the last thing I cared about.

"Please, Hales. You have to come. It's not a party without you. You're more of a people person than I am. Please?"

It's like a damn broken record. I cave. I always cave.

"Fine! I'll come. But don't expect me to stay all night."

I went back to fumbling with my clothes in the locker.

"I'm thinking of throwing a masquerade ball. So, we need to go shopping."

"I actually like that idea. Now I am more willing to go."

I dropped my towel, going full nude now before putting on my uniform again. I really hated wearing a uniform like everyone else. My parents insisted I go to a private school and said they had their reasons. When school finally ended for the day, both Luna and I went shopping, and I had already found my outfit. But shopping with Luna takes hours because she needs to try on everything there is, like we're heading to a fashion show.

When she finally found her dress, we walked out, and I saw Kaiden walking in the opposite direction from us. The look on Luna's face told me she wasn't happy about this. We stopped in our spots and looked at each other.

"We should just ignore him." Luna requested.

"Hailey?"

He already knew we saw him, so there was no way that we could avoid that.

"Too late for that now." I mumbled.

Kaiden stood there with that smug look on his face. I just wanted to wipe it off because that's the same smug that I wanted to kiss at the same time.

"What a pleasant surprise to bump into you again. It's like fate is pulling us toward each other."

He threw a sexy wink at me that sent shivers down my spine. He knew very well what kind of power he had over me. Just seeing him wink at me or a grin on his face was enough to make my knees turn to jelly. Ugh, I wanted to slap myself for turning into some love sick puppy whenever he was around. He walked over to us.

"Come on, Hailey, let's leave." Luna said.

"If you wanna leave, then go ahead and leave. I want to talk to Hailey."

This boy is bold, was all I could think. I couldn't control my face that showed the shock either.

"Well, Hailey doesn't want to talk to you, so please just get out of our faces, will you?"

"Luna, I don't recall asking you to speak for me."

She gave me a look that could kill if I allowed her to.

I continued, "you know what? You go ahead. I think I'll stay a few more minutes."

"Seriously, Hailey?" She seethed.

"Bye Felicia!" Kaiden mocked.

She gave him a dirty look before storming away and I realized we were alone now, which all of a sudden made me uncomfortable. Because when he stares at me like that, it makes me feel all squishy inside. I hated it. I didn't want to feel that way, but he was Kaiden Scott, and I love him.

"Shit, I don't know how you can keep up with her. I thought you'd get tired of her by now."

"I guess I'm used to it, so therefore, we're still friends."

I slowly picked under my nails to try to not look as awkward as I felt, but he picked up on it immediately.

"Yeah, you got a point there."

We both laughed at that.

"Alright, anyway, let's go and sit somewhere."

I nodded before we walked a few blocks to a pond near a park. We stood there in silence for a few minutes before I broke the silence.

"So. . . You said you wanted to talk to me. What is it?"

A silence fell between us again, and then I heard his sigh.

"Nothing, really. I only used that as an excuse to get you alone."

Now, I became nervous again. I've known Kaiden for over a year, but he still made me nervous in just a heartbeat. It almost felt like the beginning, when we first started hanging out. I was nervous nonstop around him. Before we knew it, the few people who were there had left, and it was only him and me now.

"So. . . What's in those shopping bags? Unless it's a secret."

"Just a few dresses I bought for Luna's masquerade ball this Friday." I answered.

"A masquerade ball, huh? Is this you asking me to be your date? Because I'd be a perfect one."

I let out a small laugh and just smiled at him. His phone started vibrating, and the mood had shifted.

"Fuck! Sorry, Hales, but I gotta go."

"Oh! Okay. No worries. I have to get home anyway."

I waved at him and started to walk away.

"Do you need a ride home?" he asked.

I turned around, and he had his arms crossed, still looking at me.

"No, it's fine. I can call my dad to pick me up."

"Are you sure?"

A part of me thought he wanted to drive me home, so our time together wasn't cut short. I was still not fully on board with being alone with him for longer than I should, or I would probably end up back in his bed without even thinking. I nodded at his question. Saying no to him was never something that happened. Deep down, I didn't want our time to end because I still had too many questions, but it wasn't a smart idea.

"Alright, see you around, Hales."

He went to walk away before he turned around again.

"Oh, by the way, Hunter wanted me to tell you that he had your car delivered back to your house."

I rolled my eyes as he walked away. I didn't understand why he kept popping up out of nowhere and then went ghost on me. God forbid he's barely able to text me back. I mean, he hadn't since I ran into him while running. When Friday came rolling in, I relaxed for that day until it was time to get ready for the ball. I took an innocent shower this time and laid out the dress that I chose. It was a long, red, silk-made dress that hugged my curves. I know I should be excited to go out, but a part of me felt a knot in my stomach that said it was a bad idea.

I touched on my makeup, which took me longer than I thought. Maybe it was because I felt uneasy about going alone, as Luna will probably end up ditching me later. Fuck, I can't believe I am doing this. I grabbed my phone and decided to text Kaiden.

Hailey: Hey, Kaiden. Remember how you said you'd be a perfect date? Want to prove it? If you

think you'd be perfect for that role, then I hope to see you at Luna's party tonight.

I let out the breath I was holding in and knew it was time to get there. When I reached the ball, it was horrible. I felt like it was something old people would love. Everyone was standing around, talking, and the atmosphere in the room felt weird. This wasn't a party for me. I stood by the drinking table, slowly sipping on my punch.

"This is so much fun, isn't it?"

Luna scared me out of my boring thoughts. Maybe it was a bit rude to say it sucked.

"Yeah, so much fun."

I let out a yawn that I tried so hard to contain.

"Cheer up, won't you? I'm sure you'll meet someone tonight."

I looked at her and she had a devious look on her face that told me she was trying to set me up with someone. Last time I let her do that, the guy was just so full of himself. I ran in the first moment I could and never heard the end of it.

"Who are you trying to set me up with this time?" I asked.

"My cousin." She gave an idiotic smile.

"And which cousin is it?"

She looked a little nervous, but her devious mind was always up to something.

"Caleb, of course. He has a big thing for you."

"LUNA! You can't be serious right now?!" I yelled.

"What's the matter?"

I went to walk away and thought maybe if I left, I could avoid him at all costs. I knew he had a huge crush on me for as long as I can remember. Anytime he is around, he flirts with me. Or can I even call it flirting? Because it's uncomfortable, but I am too nice to say anything. Luna had followed after me.

"What is wrong with Caleb?"

"He is too arrogant." I replied.

And it's true. He was extremely arrogant. He comes from money and thinks that he can buy anyone off. This is not how I want to live my life, thinking that you can solve any problem if you pay someone off.

"Who's too arrogant, baby?"

I jumped when I realized that Caleb's annoying ass had joined us. Luna was smiling and my eyes felt like they were stuck, knowing that I had to stand around him for another second. They both started talking, and I just zoned them out.

"I will leave you two love birds alone then." Luna teased.

I was suddenly snapped out of my thoughts now.

"Wait, what?"

But before I could respond, she had walked away and Caleb was smiling at me. I swear she did not just leave me with the Ken doll. I always called him Ken because he pretty much looked like him.

"You look beautiful. Maybe we should go somewhere more private."

He started walking way too close to me to the point that I had to take a step back to put more distance between us.

"Come on now, Hailey. I am not going to bite unless you let me. Don't play hard to get."

I shoved his chest a bit because he was now scaring me.

"Back up now!" I demanded.

"Or what?"

I was shocked by his response. The way he was acting was just so like him. My family came from money too. So, there was nothing that he could offer. Nothing I wanted either.

"Do you understand English or are you as stupid as you look?"

Caleb had turned around, and my eyes were now focused on Kaiden. He made it. My insides were turning to jelly again.

"My date and I are chatting. Maybe you should get the hell out of here."

Kaiden started walking closer until he was now in Caleb's face. Kaiden was so calm and collected, and Caleb looked intimidated by him.

"Nah, I am not going anywhere."

"Who even are you?" Caleb questioned.

Smug. Kaiden was so smug. God, it was so damn hot.

"I'm Kaiden. Kaiden Scott. Sound familiar?"

Caleb's face turned pale, like he had seen a ghost. But he reacted that way because Kaiden's father was not just anyone. He was the CEO of Scott Industries. He was not only powerful but super rich too and could pay anyone off if he wanted to. Kaiden's dad could literally ruin someone's life within seconds.

"If I were you, I would just beat it."

Caleb didn't hesitate. He walked so fast he left skid marks.

"I can take care of myself, you know? You must really underestimate me, the all-powerful Kaiden Scott."

He gave his infamous smile before walking closer to me until we were inches apart.

"Is that so, Hailey Davis?"

I nodded as he reached for a strand of my hair and swirled it around his finger. He had slightly yanked on it, causing me to get closer to him. He bent down until his breath was hitting my ear.

"Let's go. It's getting crowded."

He took my hand and interlocked our fingers before leading me to an empty room. It seemed like it was so fast, but also right as the air was sucked out of me. There wasn't a sound but that little bit from the ball music. I was backed up into the corner and we were so close. Was he going to kiss me?

Chapter 8

I could feel my body tensing as Kaiden disregarded any distance. It was non-existent. His chest was now smashing my breasts, but his hands stayed on his side. Our eyes locked, and he smiled at me. I didn't smile back because I was now too nervous for some reason and didn't know how to behave. The music was long gone now and the sound of my heartbeat was the only thing that could be heard. I wondered if he could hear it too? It was crazy how he had that effect on me, where I was at a loss for words. He suddenly brushed his fingertips lightly on my thigh, dragging my dress up a bit as he stared hungrily into my eyes.

Every muscle in my body tensed as his hand drew figure eights on my thigh, which caused my breathing to be hitched. For a second, it seemed I had forgotten how to breathe properly. Our eyes connected again, and I saw him biting his bottom lip. God, how badly I wanted his lips on mine at that moment. *I want him to kiss me right here, right now.*

The same way he used to kiss me while we would make love. But it didn't seem like he had any plans to do it, which made me a little disappointed. Otherwise, his lips would've been on mine by now, and I was also too shy to make the first move, even though I've done it plenty of times already. However, the situation was different now because we hadn't been together in months. I wasn't even sure what he wanted from me all of a sudden. He continued to run his fingers gently up and down my thigh.

"What are you thinking about?" His voice was so low, but I heard him perfectly.

I wasn't even sure what I was thinking. But one thing I knew was how much I wanted to grab him by his collar and invade his mouth with my tongue right then.

"Have you been with anyone since we broke up?"

The mood had officially been killed.

"Why are you asking like it's any of your business?"

"I'm just curious, that's all. No need to get all worked up."

Curious? Yeah, I'm sure he was. The question wasn't right, and I sure as hell didn't owe him that explanation. I searched his face, hoping he was just joking, but he was dead serious.

"What do you think?"

I cut past him so there was more distance between us before returning my gaze back to him.

"I think you haven't. Because when I touch you, you react the same way you did when I first touched you."

He wanted a solid answer, but I don't think I owed him that. We weren't together, and this was no break either, so would it have made a difference if I had?

"I will answer your question if you tell me first."

He sighed before sticking his hands in his front pocket.

"You sure you want to know?"

I nodded before crossing my arms and giving him my full attention. He scratched at his head a bit before finally giving me eye contact.

"Yeah, I have been with a few girls."

I was pissed. I know we had broken up four months ago, but in four months he had already been with other girls like I meant nothing. Meanwhile, I hadn't been with anyone because I was heartbroken over him.

"How many?" It slipped out of my mouth.

"Two. But it wasn't serious."

I chewed on the inside of my bottom lip. Trying not to show I was upset, but deep down, I really was. I just nodded. He walked close to me again and reached for my hand.

"None of them was like you, though." He placated.

I knew if I talked, I would probably end up saying something pretty stupid. When I looked at him now, all I could think about was him fucking other girls, which made my blood boil. His thumb ran over my lip now as he looked so lovingly at me.

"So, have you?" He asked.

I haven't been with anyone, but I wasn't going to give him the satisfaction of knowing that.

"Oh, you must have mistaken me for other girls. Because I don't kiss and tell."

I stepped back from his embrace, but he grabbed my arm, clutching me into his arms again. His emotions showed that it bothered him, which kind of made me happy.

"You look beautiful. You always do."

He changed the subject, and now the idea of me with other men was haunting him, which I was surprisingly okay with. We stared at each other as if we were competing. When we're together, it feels as if nothing around us exists anymore. As if it's just him and me.

"Really? You have?"

Perfect timing. As my phone went off and Luna's name popped up. I answered her call, and she was freaking out, trying to find me. She heard I was with Kaiden. I know she hates him, but she just freaks out every time he is around now.

"Calm down, I invited him." I said, rolling my eyes.

But apparently, that wasn't the right answer. Luna went ballistic about why it was a bad idea, but she was more pissed that he had threatened Caleb than me being with him. She was so loud that Kaiden heard her. She went on about how she was so rich and her dad is more powerful, which made Kaiden snatch the phone from my hand and put it to his ear.

"Your dad may be powerful, but my dad never goes a day without calling me. When is the last time your dad did that because he cares?"

He started laughing, and the gasp that came from her mouth made me chuckle just a bit. They went back and forth before I grabbed my phone back and ended the call.

"I swear, you two can never get along." I sighed.

"Sorry, but I don't like her. Never have and never will. She's so damn stuck up and she can't always use the 'I-broke-your-heart' excuse."

Kaiden looked at the watch on his wrist, and his demeanor changed again.

"I should leave."

"What? But you just got here."

I don't understand him lately. He seems to show up and then disappear like he's living some double life or he's about to turn into a pumpkin at midnight.

"Yeah, well, I'm not staying where I am not wanted. If you want to come with me, you can."

His words weren't convincing. It was one of the invites you make to not seem like an asshole, but really don't want them to say "yes" to. At least to me, that's what it felt like. I still don't understand why he is back, either. I didn't know what to do right now. As much as I wanted to go with him, I couldn't because I promised Luna I would be here at her party. I didn't want to be that person who betrays her best friend over a guy. Especially a guy who isn't dependable.

"Are you coming?" He woke me from my thoughts.

"No, sorry. I made a promise, so I have to stay."

But to be honest, it was an excuse to have some space. His reasoning isn't known, and I wasn't going to let him play with my heartstrings any longer.

"Don't worry, I won't hold it against you. Have fun."

I could finally breathe when he walked away. I can't expect everyone to think the same and be the same. It makes me question their thoughts. The positions we put ourselves into or the decisions that we make. However, I also don't know what others go through and maybe that's why some act a certain way. Or maybe why they react too. I didn't know that through all this, it would change me. I saw myself in a different light. Who would've known that in just a matter of months, I'd be staring at myself in the mirror and ask my own reflection, "Who am I, really?"

Who I was is someone that everyone around me didn't like. This facade I had was me just trying to please everyone. I should be asking myself why I let others walk all over me. Over and over again. Was it all for the better? But through only one set of eyes, I was perfect.

I finally zoned back in and realized I was all alone. I got back out and in time to see Kaiden walking away from Caleb. Knowing him, he had probably threatened him once again. Luna spotted me and when she reached me, I got an earful.

"I swear, Hailey, you are letting this guy completely change your attitude. He is no good for you."

"I don't think you are in any position to tell me who is good for me or not when you can't even keep a guy longer than a night."

The words came out of my mouth and I immediately wanted to take it back. It did shut her up, though. The look on her face was priceless, but this wasn't me. It was just a tad bit too mean. Sometimes, she just becomes too much and her voice is like nails on a chalkboard. I decided to walk away because I wasn't really sorry for what I said if I think about it. I got some more punch and just watched from the outside while everyone partied until ten rolled around, and I was even more bored now.

I walked over to where Luna was dancing and tapped her on the shoulder. By the look on her face, she was half in the bottle.

"I am leaving." I yelled out.

"What? But it's so early."

"Yeah, well, I am tired."

I pulled out my phone to check the time again just to prove I know how late it was.

"Okay, well, are you doing anything tomorrow?"

"Yes, I'm staying in to study since I came out tonight."

I waved at her and walked away before she had the chance to say anything back. I was not in the mood to hear her complain. I reached for my keys in my purse when I spotted a shadow, which caused me to jump and in the car window's reflection, Caleb's "Ken doll" face showed up.

"Hailey. . . "

Oh! Great! Another problem to deal with.

"You scared me. What do you want?" I asked.

"I'm really sorry about what happened before. I didn't mean to make you uncomfortable. Sometimes I can come on too strong."

"Yeah, you did. Now, if you excuse me, I have to go."

"Wait, let me make it up to you. What do you say we go for a coffee tomorrow?"

Is this boy serious? It's like he didn't get the hint.

"I don't drink coffee and I have homework to do."

I reached for my car door and quickly got in. I didn't want to give him another excuse to talk to or weirdly ask me out.

The comfort of my own house was what I needed. I had reached home and changed out of that dress and went to bed. The whole next day, all I did was study. In the evening, I noticed that my brother was downstairs, and it had been a while since I had bugged him. So, I slowly walked downstairs as he was watching a scary movie, and when the transition came. . .

"BOOO!" I yelled.

Brandon had leaped out, spilling popcorn everywhere with a loud scream.

"What the fuck, Hailey! Look what you made me do!"

"What are you, Taylor Swift now?" I burst out laughing.

At the same moment, my dad came in and started yelling at him.

"Well, you all have fun. I am going for a walk. My head hurts from studying so much."

I walked out in time for the sunset. The sky was filled with such amazing, bright colors. Purple, yellow, orange, blue and just everything that's so great. This is the type of night that calmed my soul while breathing in the fresh air. When I got around the block, I had to change my plans. I know I said I wouldn't go anywhere too far. But, sometimes when you're walking and especially if you're listening to music at the same time, you may just forget how much or how far you've been walking.

"Please, I'm begging you. Don't kill me."

A loud yell accompanied by a sob penetrated through the faint music on my earphones and landed straight in my ears. I stopped dead in my tracks when I heard that pleading voice. What the heck? I heard a man's voice not so far away, but I couldn't see anyone there. He sounded like he was in some kind of danger or something. I froze, not knowing what to do. I didn't know whether I should go and see what was going on, or if I should just mind my business and get the hell away from there as soon as possible. But what kind of person would I be if I turned a blind eye to someone who might need help?

I crept in the direction that the yell came from and looked over the brick wall. And that's when I saw them. . . The last people I'd expect to see in a situation like this one. A shudder of fear ran down my spine as I saw Hunter and Kaiden next to him, pointing a gun at a man's face. They had a bandanna over their lower face, but even with that, I knew exactly who they were. I couldn't believe my eyes. I started to think that I never really knew Kaiden after all.

Chapter 9

I was shocked. More like mortified. No fucking way this is happening. I was completely traumatized after what I had just witnessed. That couldn't be Kaiden, right? I tried to convince myself. My eyes had to play tricks on me. I panicked, and I tried to move, but I somehow couldn't. It was like my body had frozen all of a sudden. The rumors about Hunter were true after all, but I never expected Kaiden to be a part of it as well. It was Kaiden we were talking about. He didn't do stuff like this. It. . . It had to be a misunderstanding. I know what I saw, but I refused to believe that Kaiden was involved in illegal stuff.

"HELP!"

The guy called out, and he was staring right at me. Which made Kaiden and Hunter turn around to see who he was calling for help. That's when Kaiden saw me, and I knew. He knew. We knew. I could see him internally freaking out. I had to leave. So, I dashed away from there as fast as I could. But not long after, I felt a hand grab me. I slipped and scraped my knees on the ground. Kaiden lifted me up and set me in front of him.

"Are you okay?" He asked.

I couldn't look at him straight, as everything seemed so unreal. I screamed as I snatched my arm from him and felt myself literally shaking. Before I could escape, Kaiden had grabbed me and pushed back until I felt the bark of the tree on my back.

"Why the hell are you screaming?"

"What do you mean, why am I screaming? Should I be laughing after what I've just witnessed?"

I tried to break from his embrace, but he held me hostage.

"What did you witness?" He asked, like nothing had happened.

I looked at him, mad now.

"Don't you dare play stupid now."

"I don't know what you're talking about, Hales."

No, he didn't. I was about to blow a gasket now. I knew very well what he was trying to do. Rage turned into strength as I shoved him away.

"Don't try to gaslight me. You know damn well what I saw!"

"Whatever you saw, you saw wrong. Alright?"

He continued to gaslight me. The Kaiden I knew was not him. Or was I perhaps wrong? Maybe this was really him all along, and I was too blind to see the darkness in his gray eyes.

"Excuse me?"

"You heard me. You didn't see anything. So, if I were you, I'd just drop it."

He took a step back and there was this cold look on his face.

"Say it, Hailey." He demanded.

"No! I am not going to say shit. You're making me out to feel crazy for what I know I saw and heard. So no, I won't stay it, Kaiden!"

He looked at me with an annoyed expression on his face. Like I was the problem, or that I was the one who did something wrong. I was a smart person and I sure as hell won't be made out to be crazy because he didn't want to be truthful. There was no reassurance, just plain assholeness.

"You're so damn stubborn." He spoke through gritted teeth.

The way he said it was filled with so much annoyance and I didn't appreciate it.

"Do you trust me?" Kaiden asked.

I can't believe I was still standing there for this.

"Do you? Yes, or no?"

"I don't know. I want to, but I don't know you anymore. Give me one reason why I should trust you?"

He stared at me and looked me side to side like he was trying to find the best response to this.

"Because I care about you so much, and I'd never forgive myself if anything happened to you. So just please do what I say and pretend like you never saw anything."

I was a fool. I stood there quietly and looked at him, shocked.

"You're not the man I thought you were. The Kaiden I know would never hurt a soul or kill them for that fact. He would not stand here and make me out to be insane to benefit himself. I may be this innocent girl you consider me, but I am not dumb."

I brushed past him, but he grabbed me by the arm.

"Just please. I will call you later and we will talk about this, okay?"

"Don't bother. I don't want to hear from you ever again."

I snatched my arm and started running. I wanted to forget this night once and for all. I felt his eyes staring at me as I ran out of his distance. The tears had started coming out, and they weren't stopping. Everything I thought I knew felt like a lie now. When I got home, Brandon was shooting hoops outside, but like a twin intuition, he turned around and saw me.

"What the hell is up with you? I thought you were going for a walk, but you look like someone who just had their heart broken."

I said nothing. I had no words to even explain what was wrong. I didn't know how I could even explain this. Deep down, I still cared about Kaiden, so I didn't say anything about what I had witnessed. Instead, I just walked past him and ran inside. I was pretty shaken up still and didn't know how I was going to sleep peacefully tonight. I went to take a shower and stayed in the boiling hot water until my fingers turned pruned. However, that didn't help as much as I wanted it to. Exhaustion finally took over until I heard a shuffle in the room. I jumped up, frightened, when I saw Kaiden standing there.

"Kaiden! What the fuck are you doing here? How did you even get in?" I yelled.

He walked closer to me until he was a foot away from me. My body trembled, which has never happened before, especially not out of fear of him.

"I wanted to see you after what happened. I'm sorry. I know I haven't given you much of anything to trust me. I can't talk much about what you saw, but I want to answer a question you keep asking."

My eyes met his, and they showed softness.

"I miss you, Hailey. I miss everything about you. You have no idea how badly I wanted to push you against that tree earlier and kiss those perfect lips of yours. I can't restrain myself any longer, Hales. I want you. . . I need you."

I was weak. It's like I had forgotten why I was even mad when his hand grabbed the back of my neck and he forced his lips on mine. I melted like butter. His other arm snaked around my waist, hustling me against his body. Space didn't exist anymore.

"Fuck, I almost forgot how good you tasted." He whispered between our kisses.

He slowly lifted my shirt up my body when my phone started ringing.

"Ignore it."

I tried to, but at the same time, I needed to get out of this. When I reached for the phone, panic washed over me when I saw Kaiden's name pop up on the screen. I turned around and suddenly I was looking at the man who was screaming for help earlier.

"Help me!" he screamed.

I shot up from bed in cold sweat covering my body when I realized it was all just a dream. Dammit! Just when it was getting to the best part, and now I had a throbbing and warm feeling between my legs. I was way too tired to go up and clean myself. I closed my eyes and tried to fall back asleep, but then I heard a whimper. Someone was crying. I realized it was coming from Alyssa's room, which was weird. She always acted so tough and unbothered that it would be so strange to see her cry, and now I was curious. Even though we don't get along, she is still my little sister.

I made my way out of my room to hers and knocked carefully on her door.

"Are you awake?" I spoke in a loud voice.

But there was no answer, so I resorted to opening her door. When I walked in, she was on the bed with her phone in her hand, trying to act tough, but I saw her puffy red eyes.

"What do you want?" She coldly said.

"I heard you crying. What's wrong?"

However, she brushed me off.

"Oh, that must've been from the show I was watching on my phone."

To be honest, I didn't believe her. But I couldn't force her to talk about things she clearly didn't want to talk about.

"Okay, but just so you know, if you ever need to talk, I am here."

I smiled before walking out the door and returned to my room to finally get some sleep. The next day rolled around, and I decided I needed a distraction. Luna and I headed to the beach to soak in the sun. I wasn't in the mood, but she talks a lot, so I guessed I would be entertained.

"Okay, spill it. You've been acting off today and you're quite a buzzkill."

I rolled my eyes and shifted my feet. "I'm fine. Let's just relax."

"Bullshit. You've been checking your phone every two seconds. If you're expecting Kaiden to call you and tell you how much he misses and wants you back, then you'll be forever alone. This isn't some romance movie."

God, here we go again.

"The best way to move on is by giving someone else a chance, like my cousin Caleb, for example. I'm sure you'll like him more once you get to know him better."

I cringed and from the look on her face, I knew my face carried the expression of how disinterested I was.

"Yeah, no thanks. I don't want to deal with your arrogant cousin."

At the same time, my phone rang. I looked at it and couldn't help but smile.

"Who is it?" Luna asked curiously.

I pointed the screen at her to show the pop-up of Kaiden's name.

"Would you look at that? It's Kaiden. Anyways, gotta take this."

I walked off to a different area and even contemplated on actually answering. . .

I pulled on my maddest voice before finally hitting that "accept" button. "I told you I didn't want to hear from you."

"I know, but I wanted to hear your voice. I got home pretty late last night and didn't want to wake you up. Can we please meet up later?"

"I honestly don't think that's a good idea."

"Come on, Hales. I really need to see you."

"What if I don't want to see you?"

"Then I will be heartbroken. But I know you want to see me as much as I want to see you."

I won't lie. He was right, and I definitely wanted to see him, even after everything that happened. Mostly because I wanted answers, and he was the only one who could give them to me.

"Fine! But not for long. I just want some answers and that's it."

"Just put on something nice and I will see you around 6, okay?"

He hung up the phone before I could even protest. Things were so back and forth that I didn't know how to act around him now. If he could hurt other people, then why wouldn't he hurt me? No, that was crazy. How could I even think of such things? He wasn't capable of that. . . But, at the same time, he kind of was. Either way, I was still going to get my answers. The rest of the day, I kind of just pondered and over thought to myself a lot. Until the sun started setting and it was time to get ready. I settled for a short red dress that still seemed a little classy at the same time. My hair was wrapped in a messy bun and I winged the hell out of the eyeliner. If I was going to kick Kaiden out of my life once and for all, then I was going to make sure I looked fine as hell.

When six rolled around, Kaiden sent me a text to let me know he was here. I avoided my family so they wouldn't ask a lot of questions. I opened the door and saw him lean against his car while staring at his phone. As soon as he heard the clink of my heels, his eyes shot up and if I didn't know any better, you'd think he was drooling. I made my way over to him and he devoured every inch of me until I had reached him.

"Looking good, babe."

I tried to hide the blush, but that's what he did to me even when I saw him with a gun in a guy's face! What the hell was wrong with me?

"So, where are we going?"

However, my attempt to seem confident just went out the door when his smirk became the only thing on my mind. Why is he so fucking hot? ARGH!

"We're going to my dad's."

To his dad's? Did I hear him right? What kind of explanation will I get if we go there? I was so confused.

"Your Dad's? You're kidding me, right?"

Chapter 10

He just smirked at me again before interlacing his hands in mine and leading me to the passenger side of his car. He opened it and led me in, leaving me once again with millions of unanswered questions. It wasn't fair. He was stringing me along and completely ignoring what I needed to be answered. When the door shut, I watched as he walked around and got into the driver's seat. He didn't talk while he drove. I felt myself picking under my nails trying to remain calm, but the inner me wanted to smack him until he told me what I wanted to know.

"So, are you going to tell me why we're going to your dad's place instead of just staring quietly at the road?"

The tension grew, and suddenly this car seemed just a little too small for both of us.

"We were invited over. So that's why we are going." He replied.

Okay, now I was mad.

"Stop the car."

He ignored my request.

"I said stop the damn car, Kaiden!"

I refused to be dismissed. Kaiden let out an annoyed sigh before he turned the hazard lights on and went to the side of the highway. When we were at a full stop, I got out of the car and he was so quick to join me.

"You must take me for a fool, or you seriously have no respect for me whatsoever." The cars were zooming by while I yelled my words out.

"That is not true." He spoke.

"Then tell me the damn truth, Kaiden! I need to know the truth! You will not show up after a few months and talk to me a certain way. Why are you back in my life, huh? Why did you have a gun in someone's face? Why are you taking me to your dad's house after you promised we'd talk? No more dismissing me!"

Kaiden stared at me, but he didn't say anything. I took his silence as him not being honest with me. I didn't realize I was chewing on my lip as hard as I was until I tasted the copper. I walked to the passenger side and grabbed my purse before I started walking.

"Where are you going?" He yelled.

"AWAY FROM YOU!" I shouted.

I continued to walk, but could also hear his feet behind me. They were getting faster and faster and the next thing I knew, he had grabbed my arm and spun me around.

"You're acting crazy. You need to calm down."

I grabbed my arm away from him and gave him a nasty look.

"No, I am not crazy for wanting just the simplest things! I won't stand here and be constantly gaslighted and made out to be dumb. I have a mind of my own. So, if you can't be honest with me, then I am leaving!"

We were now in a staring match, but at the same time, I noticed the way his mouth was moving, like he was debating things. Was he really here for me? I mean, he was with other girls, so it's not like he was lonely. Not to mention, he was also the one who broke up with me. Now I let my insecurities get the best of me.

"Are you back just to string me along?" I asked.

He shook his head no, but still remained silent.

"Then why are you back, Kaiden? Because, to be honest, I can't stand another heartbreak from you. I won't survive. I'm still getting over the last time and here you are again, confusing my mind. When you're around, I lose sight of what's important, and that's not what I want. So again, I am going to ask. Why are you back and why were you pointing that gun at someone's head?"

He let out a long exhale before turning around with his arms on his head. Not a single sound came out of him before he started speaking.

"There are a lot of things that I want to tell you, Hailey, and it kills me to keep anything from you."

"Not good enough!" I yelled.

He was about to give me another excuse, but used his charm to get out of it. I started walking again.

"Hailey, wait!"

"NO! I am not going to allow you to talk your way out of this."

I kept walking, but he caught up to me and blocked my way.

"I'm going to tell you everything, I promise. But can we just get this dinner over with first? And then we'll have the whole night to talk."

Fuck. His eyes were pleading for me to trust him, but in my gut, I knew I couldn't. Maybe I gave him enough of a wake-up call for him to actually tell me, so I just nodded. Once again, just melting in his hands. It's like he knew he got his way because he reached for my hand and immediately interlocked our fingers to lead me back to the car. He better tell me this time or I will blow a gasket! The door shut after I had sat in the passenger seat but waited until he got in to stare out the window. We remained quiet the rest of the drive before he pulled into a driveway and entered a code to unlock the gate.

"My dad has a new girlfriend, just so you won't be surprised."

Once again, I was blindsided. I think the look on my face said everything.

"How does your mom feel about that?"

He drove into this huge garage and parked his car. He took off his seatbelt before turning to face me.

"It broke her. I had to scrape her off the kitchen floor because she was a mess. She's not over the divorce and has used alcohol as a coping mechanism, which didn't work very well. I hate how the divorce has taken my mom away. I feel like I'm the parent here."

I reached for his hand when I noticed how much pain thinking of his mom had caused him. His half-smile confirmed he needed the comfort. His dad was a filthy rich man and he basically could get away with anything. He was a nice guy. A little arrogant, of course, but someone with his kind of control needed it to keep his reputation. The garage door opened to reveal the maid, Alma.

"Kaiden? Why are you sitting in here?"

We both had gotten out of the car to go greet her.

"I'll inform your father that you're here. Hi, Hailey. It's nice to see you again."

I waved to her before she went back inside and now was nowhere in sight. I followed Kaiden, who once again interlocked our fingers until we had reached the living room. I felt so nervous now. I think even Kaiden knew when he was rubbing at my hand, trying to soothe me. His dad is very intimidating even when he is usually very nice to me, but he is also very short-tempered too.

"Don't worry, my dad has always loved you. If anything, he was mad at me for us breaking up."

He and I both. At that moment, his dad came walking in with a blond girl who seemed to be half his age. Her stare was worse than his, but unlike her, he had a smile on too.

"Are you both gossiping about me?"

I felt myself scratching my neck, not knowing what to say. I don't know what her issue was, but she was really giving me a look like I had just ruined her favorite purse.

"Thank you both for coming. Hailey, I missed seeing your face around here."

Kaiden had scoffed at that like he was now angry.

"It's not like I had a choice, right?"

They exchanged a harsh look with each other. He definitely gets the intimidation from his father.

"Anyway, this is Charlotte, my beautiful girlfriend. Honey, meet my son Kaiden and his umm. . ." He looked between us, trying to catch the vibe. "Ex-girlfriend, Hailey."

Now things felt really awkward because why would he bring his ex-girlfriend to a family dinner? It made no sense, right?

"It's a pleasure to finally meet you, Kaiden. You're as handsome as your dad has said."

She could not be serious right now. The way she looked at him told me she had those fuck me eyes. I am a girl, so I know those eyes. Hell, any female knows those eyes. Now I felt like I needed to stake my claim. I wrapped my hands around his arm and her smile was as fake as her lips.

"Your father never stops bragging about you, and I see why now."

She hadn't even acknowledged that I was there yet, and I had a feeling that she probably wouldn't even do it.

"We're pretty hungry. Can we just eat now?"

"Don't be rude."

Uh oh, they were now playing a game of who's bigger. Both Charlotte and I got uncomfortable. He dropped my hand to perfect his stance. Charlotte ended up breaking the staring contest and lead us into the dining hall. I was hungry but now my nerves were up, so I ended up playing with the food on my plate. The tension was thick, but I kept catching Charlotte staring at him.

"So. . . How are you doing, Hailey? It has been a while since I've seen you. Is school going well?"

I placed my fork down to give him my attention.

"Yeah, it's going great. I am actually valedictorian and graduating with a 4.5 GPA. So, I have been able to relax for the rest of the school year because I have all the credits I need and more."

He had the proud parent's look on his face.

"You're going to college, right? Do you need any letters of recommendation? I'd be happy to do so."

"No need to. I actually have a handful of offers. However, my dream college offered me a chance to start earlier. So, I may take it."

"Oh really? And what college is that?" He asked.

"Columbia."

There was that smile again, but I kind of felt an uncomfortable feeling next to me. I assume Kaiden forgot that I wanted to go there. I mean, when we were dating, I started looking for colleges around here and I got accepted, but that all changed when we broke up.

"That is an excellent choice. I went there myself, actually."

"I thought you wanted to go to Stanford?" Kaiden intruded into the conversation.

I was hoping he wasn't going to bring that up. It wasn't even on my top five choices, but love makes you do crazy things.

"Yeah, I did at first. However, I changed my mind when I realized there is no reason to stay in California anymore."

He got the hint. He knew exactly what I meant by that, and I think his dad understood that as well. Kaiden looked at me with pleading eyes but also realized that he can't make me stay either. He has given me no reason to even reconsider.

"Can we please not discuss school or work at the dinner table?" Charlotte chimed in.

"You know, I am curious about what you do for work." Kaiden directed his question toward Charlotte and it was the million-dollar question, too. Because she looked like a gold digger.

"I'm a model. A supermodel." She took a sip of her champagne.

"Oh really? Then you may know my mom, Chantelle Davis. She's a pretty well-known supermodel."

Her eyes had widened. For the first time, she acknowledged I was at the table.

"That's your mom?"

I nodded my head while putting a green bean in my mouth. She was amazed for a moment, but then went back to her envious look. Maybe it was all the Botox in her face.

For the rest of the dinner, Kaiden's dad was the one who talked the majority of the time, and we were just there listening to him. The one thing I had noticed was that Charlotte was staring at Kaiden the entire time. Now that was disrespectful. No regard for her his dad at all. After dinner, Kaiden's dad wanted to have a word with him, so I toured the house and found a balcony to have some fresh air. This night was a mixture of confusion and awkwardness all in one tiny bubble. I also didn't want to be alone with Charlotte and pretend we could tolerate each other.

I know I told myself I needed to set boundaries, but he made me weak. I was the middle school girl who just got her first kiss, kind of weak. Or hiding while my friend told a guy I liked him kind of weak. Kaiden Scott clouded my judgment all together. He promised me answers, and I hope I'll get them.

"There you are." I jumped out of deep thoughts to Kaiden showing up behind me. "What are you doing out here?"

He walked closer to me, but there was still some space between us.

"Did you kill him?"

It slipped out of my mouth. Not knowing was worse than knowing. He let out a deep breath, and I was expecting any type of reluctance, but there wasn't one.

"No. I am not a murderer, Hailey. You, of all people, should know that."

I turned around to face him.

"Then why did you hold a gun to that guy's head? Why did I witness you doing that?"

"I tag along with Hunter. But I only go for the thrill of living life on the edge, but he does it all."

Hunter? HUNTER! The rumors were true. I swallowed the frog in my throat, knowing if I was alone, what if he comes after me?

"It's nothing you need to worry about, though, and I am so sorry you had to witness that."

The silence lingered on a little longer than I wanted it to, but that wasn't the only question I wanted to get an answer for. I turned around again and placed my hands on the balcony walls.

"Why are you back in my life? What do you want?"

My heart had skipped a beat, or maybe two, as Kaiden stepped closer and closer until I felt his hard chest pressing against my back.

"I love you, Hailey."

His hot breath hit my neck, and the hair stood right up.

"I have loved you ever since I tasted those juicy lips of yours. Us breaking up was the worst thing I did, and when Hunter told me he saw you, I couldn't help but remember some of our moments together. I want you. I want us. And I'll spend the rest of my life making it up to you."

My breath became ragged hearing all that.

"I know all you can think about is the fact that I've been with other girls, but they weren't you. They aren't even close to being you and the guilt ate me away. So, I thought of you. Fuck, Hailey, just thinking about being inside you drove me insane."

His hand rubbed my arm.

"The things I'd do to you right now. . . " He said as he swept my hair to one side and leaned forward, pressing his lips against my neck.

"My favorite smell is you. And fuck, you look so damn delicious."

Goosebumps quickly rose all over my skin as I felt his warm breath cascade down my body. My knees wanted to buckle. I was weak for Kaiden Scott. He lingered his hand down my arm and continued to my hips until he got to the hem of my dress.

"Tell me if you want me to stop, and I will." He whispered in my ear.

But I said nothing because the shy girl inside me was too ashamed to admit that I'd have him right here if he wanted. His tongue invaded my neck as he slid his hand under my dress, pulling it upward.

"Tell me you want me to continue."

Fuck! He will stop if I don't say anything.

"Please continue," I whimpered.

His tongue licked alongside my ear as he slowly blew, causing a warmth between my legs.

"Don't make a sound."

He had pulled my thong to the side, and I felt his finger slide down my folds and my body on cue had leaned against his chest.

"Fuck, you're so wet for me. I don't know how I am going to contain myself."

He found my clit and slowly began to circle his finger, and now my entire body was on fire with just one touch. He went slow, and I was wanting more to the point I started moving my hips, but he used his other hand to stop my movements.

"Kaiden. . . " I moaned.

But he shushed me, telling me to stay quiet.

He continued at his slow pace, but I wasn't ready as he inserted his fingers inside my wet core while his thumb was still assaulting my clit. His pace quickened and now I couldn't handle it. It's like he studied my body and knew exactly what to do to get me to my finish before I had a chance to soak it in. My body was already about to unfold. My aroused nipples were poking outside my dress, showing exactly how horny I was now. Kaiden's pace got quicker, and now I was about to lose it. I was literally losing it! His heavy breath in my ear and how fast his fingers were plunging in and out of my opening, I felt my walls contracting and I knew I wasn't able to stay quiet.

Kaiden used his other hand to cover my mouth when I let out a scream that was muffled, but still loud enough that anyone could hear it. He teased my sensitive clit as my orgasm still was active. It was so amazing, but now I was sensitive to where it hurt that I pulled myself away from him and held myself against the balcony, trying to catch my breath. My legs were shaking still while I was coming down from a high. He stared at me with so much hunger, and I could see his dick pressing hard against his pants. It seemed like his pants were about to rip with how hard he was. My orgasm was all over his fingers and when he realized I was looking at his hand, he brought his hand up to his mouth before sucking every inch of my cum from his fingers.

He must know how much that turned me on, because I was ready to risk getting caught just to feel it again. He let out a sexy laugh.

"Are you alright?"

Is he really asking me that?

"I'm just gonna go and wash my hands and then we will head out, okay?"

I nodded, and now I was breathing a sigh of relief. What the hell just happened and could it please happen again? I waited a good ten minutes and realized he wasn't back, so I decided to go find him. When I went to the bathroom to see what was taking so long. I saw him and his dad's girlfriend standing pretty close to each other, almost as if Kaiden had trapped her against the wall. An uneasy feeling set in my stomach. While it looked wrong in so many ways, I didn't know what to think at that moment. He had turned around and the "oh fuck" look appeared on his face while she had a victory smile.

"Hailey, it's not what it looks like."

But even I wasn't that dumb to believe such a line. Usually, when someone says that, it's because it is what it looks like.

"Nothing happened. Tell her, Charlotte."

But she didn't answer. She just smiled like she was hoping I would believe it.

"Why do you even have to explain yourself to your ex?"

This was way too much for one night. He was single, and honestly, I don't want the drama.

"I think I'm going to call my brother to pick me up instead."

I didn't want to be here, so I walked out and almost made it outside, but Kaiden had caught up to me.

"Hailey, wait!"

I stopped and turned around to face him.

"She came onto me, and I pushed her off. That's all that happened. You have to believe me."

In most cases, you shouldn't believe a line like this, but from the way she was staring at him all night, I knew he was telling the truth. Sadly enough, I trust him and after what we just did, I don't think he'd want someone else. He told me he loved me, after all.

"Oh my God, this is fucked up! I think you should tell your dad about it."

"I will, if she ever does it again. I threatened her, so hopefully she backs off."

He reached for my hand and we lingered there.

"Anyway, you wanna get the hell out of here?"

I let out a laugh and just nodded. I wanted this strange night to end already and just be with him. He was Kaiden. He was my Kaiden. However, even with all this, Charlotte was on a mission. Kaiden became her mission. Like making up lies in order to tear the bond he and his dad had. It was a sick obsession. It would ruin more than you know, and here I was just helpless. The drive home wasn't awkward anymore. Now that I know the truth, maybe things could be different. He pulled up to my house and got out with me.

"Sorry about tonight, but I am also not sorry."

We both laughed, knowing what sins we just committed.

"Goodnight, Kaiden."

I placed a kiss on his cheek, but he held onto me like he didn't want this night to end.

"Hailey, why did you change your mind about going to Stanford?"

This must have really been bugging him. I exhaled deeply.

"Kaiden, the only reason I was going there was because I wanted to stay near you. We broke up, so there was no need for me to go there anymore."

"So, you're moving to New York, then?"

I nodded at him and now that awkwardness was there again.

"For the next four years, yes."

"You realize four years isn't four weeks, right?"

My eyes met the back of my head.

"I realize that, but it's not that long either."

Was this his way of saying he was going to miss me or he didn't want me to leave because maybe we could try again? But do I really want to make my decision based on if our relationship will make it this time around? My life shouldn't revolve around Kaiden Scott. But somehow it still did.

"Goodnight, Hailey."

"Wait! Will I see you again, or was this it?" I asked.

His mouth formed a smirk, and he walked back to his car.

"Maybe."

He started laughing, so I took that as a yes. I just thought to myself as he drove off that I was about to open my heart again and give him every inch of me again. I was about to ride this rollercoaster once again, knowing damn well he may break my heart again.

Chapter 11

Here's the thing about this innocent act that I have. People love it. They adore it. They never blame because that's not who you are and who they know. Some will go to the ends of the earth defending you because you never showed a bad bone in your body. If you think about it then, we are all fools. We are just puppets in a game and sometimes things are way out of our control. However, some are better at hiding it than others. For me, it's written on my face. Like an open book. I am so easily predictable, but maybe it's the facade that I put up. I am not allowed to show anything else. Anything out of the normal, people want to consider it a phase or maybe I am sick. Yet, the thing about control is knowing when it's appropriate or when you're out of line. So, when I see people like Hunter or Luna, I envy them.

They have no regret for doing anything in their lives. They own up to it because that's just who they are, and no one expects anything out of them as they do with me. Such a strange thing to be envious of, but this good girl image that was painted on me wasn't something I wanted.

I, for once, didn't know for a while the person who was inside me. Like a wild animal, finally seeing the wild and discovering new things. That I'd do so many things and be happy about it. It shocked me and even I was completely stunned. Like how could in just a few months my entire life be flipped upside down with so many different emotions and situations that if someone would have told them to me at this moment, I'd call them a liar. Because even I didn't know I was capable of doing such things. It was a light that was switched on that had never been lit before. My thoughts referred back to last night.

What Kaiden and I did on that balcony was something I'd never done before, but it was the rush and the excitement of how we could've gotten caught that led me to finish so amazingly. From the look on his face, I can say he didn't know I'd enjoy that as much as I did. A slam on the desk woke me up. I didn't even realize I had fallen asleep. I looked around frantically and realized that I was in the library.

"Why the hell were you sleeping?" Luna asked.

I slightly stretched and wiped the side of my mouth that was drenched with some drool. Some damn daydreaming, I was doing.

"I didn't go to bed until late last night. I went to dinner with Kaiden at his dad's house."

But just like I expected, she wasn't happy with that. Come to think of it. She never really liked us together, even before we broke up. Personally, I think it's because I spent more time with him or that we couldn't be the pretty single best friends who do everything together. Maybe it was something more, but she would never get that deep. For someone like Luna, you'd never see her be vulnerable. I can count on one hand the times I see her cry. If anything, she smiles and then tries to ruin someone's life.

"Please tell me you two are not back together?"

There it was. The judgment that seethed out her mouth.

"No, we aren't, but his dad invited him over for dinner to meet his new girlfriend. He didn't want to go alone, so he asked me to go with him. I mean, more like I didn't have a choice because he told me when we got into the car."

"His dad has a new girlfriend! Spill the tea."

She had her hands under her chin, staring at me like I was about to give her the gossip she needs to fill her evil soul.

"Yep, and she's like twenty-five years old too. You should've seen the way she was staring at Kaiden. I don't think she blinked once the entire time. Right in front of me, and honestly didn't care that I was there."

I thought we were going to move past things, but unfortunately Luna had this face on hers that just showed she doesn't agree with Kaiden or I. She pretended to check her phone and made excuses to why she needed to go. Yet the dissatisfied look never left her face. It was best that I didn't stress about her because she will never agree with me. I relaxed, leaning back in my chair and shut my eyes again. Before I knew it, the exhaustion took over, and I was in this trance. Just dreaming away.

"Hailey, wake up!"

I jumped up after being woken up.

"Kaiden, what are you doing here?"

I sat up and rubbed my eyes so they could adjust to his figure. He sat down in the chair that Luna had left with that smug on his face.

"I was in the area and thought I'd visit you. Then, I ran into Luna, who told me you may still be here and I see why now."

We were back at the staring match and now my mind was going to different places. He moved closer, but grabbed my hand and lifted me up.

"Come with me. We're going somewhere. And before you ask. I am not telling you, so just trust me."

Before I could say anything, he pulled me into a private area of the library and trapped me between the sections of fantasy and history.

"Kaiden-"

I tried to talk, but he put his finger to his mouth to tell me to shut up. His eyes turned dark when he looked at me and I felt it down my spine.

"Do you know how much you turn me on in this school uniform?"

He reached for the buttons and there wasn't a second in between him sliding his finger down and now my bra was fully exposed.

"Oops."

His sadistic grin came back, and it was hotter than ever. He reached down to my ear, and I felt his warm breath, and now I had those dirty thoughts back in my head.

"Did you enjoy our little moment on the balcony last night?"

Silence erupted as he snaked his hands around my waist, pulling me closer to him. Like one night of weakness, just unleashed a lifetime of hot moments like this. His eyes met mine and for a moment, I was melting. I was at his beck and call. His thumb still on my lip entered my mouth and on cue, I sucked on it. Then it hit me that we were in a very public library and had a higher chance of someone seeing us. I distanced us a bit and started reaching for the buttons on my shirt again.

"Kaiden, not here. Someone will see us."

That didn't stop him. He stopped my hands from closing my shirt and pulled me to him while he placed his lips on mine. My back was so pressed up against the bookshelf, I was knocking them off the shelf.

"Hailey?"

"Yes, Kaiden?"

"Hailey, it's not Kaiden."

My eyes shot open and now I was staring at Zane.

"Fuck, it was just a dream."

I placed my head on the table and realized how soaked my underwear was.

"Looks like I interrupted a very interesting dream."

The embarrassment had washed over my face, which caused him to laugh. I wanted to die. If lightning were to strike down, I swear it would be the perfect timing.

"Well, anyway, are you going to lunch?" Zane asked.

I shot up and reached for my phone and realized it was already noon. I gathered my books and ran even though I had no reason to do that. Maybe it was more to get rid of these thoughts from my head. Have you ever thought that maybe someone is just out of your league? Sometimes those insecurities get to me. The things that I've learned and now looking at Kaiden just made me think that maybe we are two different people on different pages, but when we're together, I can't think of being without him. However, the future is unclear. I should be able to see it, but when it comes to him, it's unpredictable. Maybe I was too young to know what I wanted, or maybe I just didn't want to know everything right away.

Soon school came and ended and I was ready to just put this entire day ahead of me.

"Hey, you want to come over?"

Luna was leaning against the lockers, staring at her phone.

"Sure, just let me get out of this uniform first."

I headed for the restroom and put on my backup outfit. God forbid, I didn't want to wear that dreadful outfit. It made me think why she was inviting me over, even though she couldn't wait to get away from me earlier because I was talking about Kaiden. When we got to her house, we went to her playroom, which had a pool table, and it was usually what we did if we're not doing our normal gossiping.

"Hello, ladies." Caleb spoke up.

I looked at Luna and saw the look on her face and then back at him. This bitch really set me up to come here thinking I would fall for this cargo pants-wearing guy who made my skin crawl.

"I swear, I didn't know that he was here." She contended.

Like she could read my mind. I bit on my lip and just gave her the death stare. I don't know why she is so hell-bent on me dating Caleb like he isn't the most arrogant person I know.

"She really didn't know. I actually came to talk to your father about something, but your housekeeper told me he's not home."

They exchanged a few words, and I focused on the wall so that I could stop eye contact with everyone. She threw her bag down before turning back to me.

"I am going to get changed. I will be right back."

I grabbed her arm before she walked away and pulled her closer to me.

"Please don't leave me alone with him." I begged.

"Why not? It's not like he's going to eat you up or something."

She pulled away from my hand as much as I tried to keep her there, but eventually, she was gone and the tension just grew in the room. I turned around to Caleb, who was staring at me with a smile on his face.

"How are you, Hailey?"

I smiled at him before I set my things down and walked over to the pool table so I was not standing around awkwardly. I heard footsteps while I was racking the balls.

"Can I ask you something?" He asked.

"Ask me what?"

I once again started doing who-knows-what to avoid eye contact with him.

"Are you dating someone at the moment?"

Great, he's going to ask me out. I could feel it. I don't understand his obsession with me, but it's been an ongoing issue.

"Why are you asking me that?"

His face softened up and here it goes again.

"Because I would like to take you out on a date."

There it was. I swear this dude could never take a hint, and you'd think seeing Kaiden with me would make him back off. Maybe it was something that made him excited. I sighed and I think it was written on my face.

"Just one date. That's all I'm asking for to show you I am a good guy." He pleaded.

I shook my head, trying to find a way to let him down easily.

"Come on, Hailey. Just one date. If you still don't like me afterward, then I promise I will never bother you again."

He seemed genuine and that good girl inside me just wanted to give him a chance. I mean, it wouldn't change my mind, but maybe this time he will take the hint.

"Fine. One date, but that's all."

He grinned like a kid who just got a piece of candy and it kind of frightened me. There wasn't anything that attracted me to him. If anything, I was more repulsed than anything. My mind went back to Kaiden. He lives in my head rent-free as always. Wondering what he was doing and how he was doing. He never leaves, but he was always up to something since discovering his secret. I remember how many secrets he had and some of them had different intentions. Some were good, and some I felt like were out of spite. Some even made me question everything. Like a kiss. A kiss with ill intentions.

Chapter 12

Kaiden

Decisions… Sometimes they're for the good and some are for the bad. The truth is sometimes harder than the lie, and I just wanted to protect her. The truth is, if she knew, then I don't know how she could ever look at me the same. I mean, even now her eyes don't look at me the same. I see desire, but I don't see trust anymore. A slap on my back woke me out of my thoughts.

"Bro, you were daydreaming again." Hunter's voice jolted me back to present.

I came to it and remembered where we were.

"Yeah, I zoned out. I have a lot on my mind."

His attention was on me now. Sooner than later, he is going to find out, so I might as well tell him.

"I told Hailey the truth."

The concern turned sour, and he was now pissed. He didn't want anyone to know, but I'd lose her again if I kept lying. My biggest regret was not telling her from the beginning. Maybe it would have saved a lot of heartaches trying to put things back together now.

"What the fuck did you say?" Hunter yelled.

A sound of a scream and a figure came running toward us, and when it got closer, I realized it was Alyssa. What the fuck is she doing on this side of town? She ran into my arms in complete panic.

"What's going on?" I asked her.

"There are some men chasing me."

Hunter and I both looked up, and there they were. As soon as they saw us, they froze in their tracks.

"Take the brat home. I will handle them." Hunter said.

By the look on Alyssa's face, she was offended, but I wanted to avoid his wrath. So, I placed my hand on her back and led her away. When we got to my car, I knew I had to call Hailey.

"What are you doing?"

"I am calling Hailey, and then I'm taking you home."

Panic washed over her face before she grabbed my phone from my hands.

"No, please don't. She will freak out and I can't go home or my parents will know I am cutting classes. Please, Kaiden!"

She begged, and I felt bad, but a part of me knew this was a bad idea. But I was once the kid who ditched school too. I let out a sigh and buckled.

"Fine, but once school ends, I am taking you back and you have to tell her. If your sister finds out, I kept you from school. All kinds of thoughts will run through her mind and she will have my head."

She smiled and agreed and before you know it, we were heading to my place. If things weren't awkward as it is, she unfolded and told me everything that happened, why she cut school and ended up where she was. Apparently, she's been getting bullied and ended up doing something she regrets that made it all worse. Teenager problems. Alyssa started crying when she finished, so I walked over and hugged her to comfort her. Why does kindness turn into something else for others?

"Thank you for listening to me. You're a good guy."

I smiled at her and gave her a pat on the back, but in a swift moment, she reached up and kissed me with her hands, holding my head. What the hell! I pushed back from her grasp and put some distance between us. I stood there in complete shock and wiped my mouth, trying to comprehend what the hell had just happened.

"What the fuck are you doing? You're a damn minor and I sure as hell didn't send those mixed signals to you."

She looked embarrassed and like she couldn't believe what she did, but honestly, I think she knew exactly what she was doing.

"I'm sorry. I got caught up in the moment." She cried.

I shook my head and reached for my keys.

"Hailey is going to be furious when she finds out. Come on, I am taking you home."

She grabbed my arms, stopping me from heading inside the car.

"Oh my God, no! You cannot tell Hailey about this. She will hate me!"

"You should've thought about that before kissing me."

Alyssa tugged at her sleeves and let out a prolonged sigh.

"Please. I will tell her, okay?"

A mess was being created, but I didn't want to mess things up again. I just got Hailey back and now her little sister kissing me was the icing on the cake. I was reluctant because their relationship was always something on rocks as is. There was some kind of unspoken rivalry. I know Alyssa wanted to be her big sister and achieve things that are hard for her. Now hearing this made me feel bad, but it was no excuse either.

"Fine, you'll tell her."

I left her there looking ashamed, but I needed to get as far away from this situation. My phone started ringing and realized it was my dad.

"Yeah?" I answered.

"Are you busy right now?"

"Not really. Why?"

"Could you come to my office? I need to have a word with you?"

"What is it now?"

"Just come to my office, will you?"

The line clicked before I could object. Great, now I have to deal with him too. Alyssa got into the car, and it was quiet the entire time. Last thing I needed was for her parents to see it's me dropping her off and accuse me of something I didn't do. It was messy. So, I dropped her off at the corner of her street. When the car stopped, she looked at me, but I reached over and opened the door, so she knew I didn't want to talk. She showed some remorse, but didn't try anymore. She got out and didn't say anything. I waited until I knew she was close to her house before leaving and heading to my dad's office. When I got there, I felt the tension in the room like this wasn't going to be a pleasant conversation. His face when I opened the door showed exactly how it felt. He was pissed.

"What do you want? I have to meet Hunter soon. So, if you could hurry, that would be great."

He slammed down the papers in his hands and shot those daggers at me. He made his way around and leaned against his desk.

"What's your deal? Charlotte took your wallet and ran away?" I let out a laugh, but that just made him angrier.

"Speaking of Charlotte. She told me what you did."

"What I did? What the fuck are you talking about?"

"Don't act like you don't know what I'm talking about." Venom shot out his mouth.

"Now I am really lost. So can you just stop with the riddles and tell me what the fuck you're talking about?"

"My girlfriend, of all people, really? What the hell is wrong with you, Kaiden? What did you think, huh? That she would actually sleep with you?"

I took a step back, completely stunned by his accusations. The more I questioned, the more he got angry, and if I wasn't his son, I am sure he would have had my head against the wall right now.

"Hold on! What exactly did she say to you?" I questioned.

"She told me you came onto her in the bathroom."

This fucking bitch. I threatened her, and she wants to make my dad hate me now.

"This is unacceptable behavior, Kaiden, and it better never happen again, or I will cut you off."

"You're fucking kidding me, right? Your bitch of a girlfriend is lying to you because there is no way I'd want someone so fake that she is recyclable."

His hands reached for my jacket and now we were against the wall. His hot breath hit my face while the anger that was let out had flooded the room, making it hard to breathe.

"Don't you ever speak about her like that again, do you hear me?"

For all the times that he wasn't there for me, you'd think that he would always have my back. Now the temper he had passed down to me finally came out. I pushed him off and pushed him against the wall.

"Really? You're going to believe your gold-digging girlfriend over your son? What? So, you didn't neglect me enough and you want to never believe me now? I'd never do that, but apparently, you think so low of me that you actually believe her?"

Our breaths were loud in sync. I released his shirt and took a few steps to try to calm down.

"You don't believe me, do you?" I asked calmly.

My dad hesitated for a second before replying.

"No, I don't. Because I know damn well what kind of guy you are and it's the reason, you couldn't keep a good girl like Hailey."

I was too stunned to speak. He wanted to shoot daggers at me that maybe I should've fucked his girlfriend, so at least when he accused me, it would be true. There was no point in fighting, because what was the point? I mean, it's not like we had the greatest relationship to begin with. I reached into my back pocket and reached for my wallet. I pulled out his credit card and threw it to the ground. I didn't need his money because I was doing fine on my own helping Hunter out. The only thing my old man gave me was trust issues, distance, and his money. There was no love or care in the world. So, I cut the only thing we had tied together. His eyes followed the piece of plastic as it made it thump on the ground. I met his eyes once more, and they softened up right before I turned around and didn't look back. He must be mistaken, thinking I need him. I once did, but I wasn't eight anymore wondering why Daddy isn't paying me any attention or why he wasn't at my practices or games cheering me on. I was just an heir to him. To take care of this fucking business and make him look good. I sat in my car in silence, just taking everything in.

It was like being rejected all over again. I didn't even notice the tear escaping my eye like it had a right to come out. I won't cry for him, and I sure as hell won't give him that satisfaction. Under the fancy ties and his 401ks. He was nothing. No good qualities. The way I am, I got from my mom and he ruined her. I won't let him do to me what he did to her. I wiped the tear away before turning the car on and leaving it all behind for now. Once again, hiding what Hailey will probably not know. I don't need her pity, because that's just who she is. Caring. But I don't need that look on her face. I pulled up to the bar on the 60th street that was hidden in a garage. This was where all of Hunter's gang members were if he needed to conduct a certain business. I turned the ignition off and made my way inside to find Hunter drinking.

"What the hell is up with you?"

But that was a loaded question. There was a lot.

"Don't even ask."

I took the beer out of his hands and took a swig before handing it back. I wasn't much of a drinker, but when I did it, it was nice to escape for just a moment.

"Where's the brat?"

"I drove her home. You won't believe the shit she pulled. I was just trying to be a nice guy, but this brat decided me being nice was a window for her to kiss me."

Hunter's eyebrows shot up and was just as shocked as I was.

"Are you fucking serious? She's a minor. Your ass is going to jail." He let out a small laugh.

That eventually turned into an uncontrollable laughter that the beer seemed to spill out his mouth.

"This isn't funny, man. First, my dad's girlfriend tries her shit and makes him believe it was me who came onto her and now this? I swear, I can't catch a break."

He stopped laughing to be serious for a minute and stared at me, trying to keep it together.

"I want to feel for you, but someone come get him. He needs to go to jail."

The laugh got louder, which now annoyed me. I took the rest of his beer and downed it because I will probably not live this down.

"Okay, okay. I'm done now. But really? Your dad didn't believe you? That's some fucked up shit, man."

"I know, right? But whatever. I don't care about him nor that bitch right now. I am worried about how Hailey will react when Alyssa tells her about the kiss."

He gave me a look, which meant I was about to get the "Hunter wisdom".

"Man, I am no expert in relationships, but you never let a woman translate information like that. They will twist it. Didn't you tell me they have a rocky relationship?" He paused to take another sip of his beer. "Listen, if she could go ahead and kiss her sister's ex-boyfriend. Then trust me, she's capable of deception." He continued.

There was the wisdom for someone who's never been in a relationship. Makes more sense than anyone could imagine, but something inside me felt like she wouldn't do that. We don't have any issues, so why would she do that knowing I didn't want her?

"Look, she's just going through some shit at school and she was sad. It was just the moment. I'm sure she'll do the right thing. But maybe you're right. I should be the one to tell Hailey, just in case."

"Just remember, don't drop the soap. Arrest this man!"

He went on laughing some more and now I was over this shit. This is my best friend right here. I guess he wouldn't be my best friend if he didn't laugh at a serious situation. Now my mind was racing, hoping he wasn't right, but maybe I need to be the first one to say something to Hailey. Words get lost in translation all the time. The universe is finding ways to keep us apart. But I won't let it. Because there is nothing that will get in our way to our happy ending.

***

Hailey

I let the day drag on and went ahead and started getting ready so I can get rid of Caleb once and for all. There are two different types of people who have money. Those that rub it in others' faces and those who remain humble. I guess you can tell who is who. I never believed in that because it's my parents with the money. I slipped on a really simple floral dress that sat in the middle of my thighs and just let my hair flow normally. I didn't try very hard for obvious reasons. I couldn't believe that I even agreed to this. I was entertaining it for whatever reason, I guess. I was startled with the door aggressively opening and Alyssa standing a few feet away with a cold expression on her face.

"Ever heard of knocking? It comes in handy."

She stared at me, still with nothing behind those eyes, like she was ready to finally win. I don't understand, but I was prepared. Or so I thought.

"Sorry, but I need to tell you something."

Her arms folded across her chest and now the tension in the room got thicker.

"Tell me what? Can you please hurry, though? I have to leave soon."

I heard her exhale, and I looked up from my phone and the look on her face had changed.

"Leave where?" She asked.

"On a date with Luna's cousin, but anyways, he won't stop bugging me unless I give him one date."

There was no chance that I could read her. The wheels were turning and if I knew back then what I knew now. I'd tell myself I couldn't trust her. I mean, how could I?

"Where are you guys going?"

"The theaters on main or something like that. Look, we will talk later. I really have to go now."

I zoomed past her, hoping not to engage in any conversation anymore. Today has been a weird day as it is and the last thing I wanted was to deal with my little sister who wouldn't care if I fell off the edge of the earth. I was sure I'll come back and find exactly what she was up to. When I got to the theaters, Caleb was there waiting for me. He wasn't a bad-looking guy. He had the Hawaiian look on him. If only his ego wasn't the size of Texas, maybe I would be more willing to try this out.

"You look beautiful, Hailey." He walked over and pulled me into an uncomfortable hug.

"Thanks. We should go inside before the movie starts."

I went straight for the door so that I didn't have to be on this date longer than I was. It hadn't even been a few minutes and the knot in my stomach had tightened and I was feeling uncomfortable. When we walked in, I realized it was empty. Only people that were there looked to be the workers.

"Where is everyone?"

"Not here. I booked the theater for just the two of us."

There it was. The not-so-humble rich guy who thinks he can buy my affection with his money. I rolled my eyes and shifted in my spot, wishing this would be over already.

"I just wanted it to be cozier for us with no one around."

Now, I wanted to run. If he thinks that just because we're alone, I would like him more, then he was mistaken. He grabbed my hand and led me to the seat. I felt myself on the edge of my sleep and not even concentrating on the movie because my thoughts went to Kaiden. This is how this "date" became a tad bearable. When it ended, he turned over to me, asking if I enjoyed the movie but couldn't bring myself to lie. So, I nodded and looked for the exit.

"You don't have to lie. The look on your face says otherwise. If you want, we can watch something more romantic."

Caleb had that grin on his face, like this was his plan all along. I do like romance movies, but he wasn't going to know that and give him another reason to spend more time with me. One good thing about movies is that you don't have to look or talk to each other.

"No thanks, I think I am just ready to go home now. It's getting late."

Apparently, he didn't like that answer.

Chapter 13

However, he didn't fight me. We didn't make one sound until we got outside the theater.

"Well, thanks for the evening. I am going to head home." I went to walk away, but he grabbed my hand to stop me.

"Already? The date is not even over. We still have dinner and then maybe afterward we can go for a walk on the beach."

He didn't tell me that there was going to be more than this. I tried to search my mind for any excuse to get out of this, but came up short handed. He just won't take a hint.

"I'm sorry, Caleb, I didn't think there was more and I need to go home and study now."

"Really? Studying on a Saturday night?"

The "T" rolled off his tongue with annoyance and now I felt a little guilty, but I wasn't really lying either. I mean, all I do is pretty much study.

"I'm sorry." I apologized.

I once again tried to leave, but his words stopped me.

"Hailey, you agreed to this date, remember? And I've already booked the table for us."

I rolled my eyes at how much of a tantrum he was throwing right now. Like a little kid who doesn't get his way. The disgust was starting to show me exactly why I could never date a silver spoon guy like him. Hell, if Luna wasn't his cousin, they'd be perfect for each other.

"Then just cancel it. It's not that hard. I mean, a kid could do it."

Kaiden's voice sprung from behind me and I thought to myself, great. Just fucking great! He stared past me and now there was a death glare match going on between him and Caleb.

"Kaiden, what are you doing here?" I was surprised.

"I could ask you the same thing."

My eyes were on him, but he was still killing Caleb next to me. The way he talked to me was cold, like I did something wrong, but it was most likely from him being jealous. I was more in shock than anything because who could ever get out of this situation?

"She's on a date with me, which you're interrupting, by the way."

Kaiden walked closer, with only me in the middle of them. The steam coming off his body was about to blow a vessel.

"No one's talking to you, so keep your mouth shut! Hailey, let's go." He demanded.

"I don't know who the hell you think you are, but Hailey isn't going anywhere with you. I will take her home after our date is finished."

The way Caleb seethed made things even worse. I went to talk, but in just a flash an arm flew past me, making an impact on something hard. Caleb was now on the ground, holding his face.

"If you think—"

But I couldn't continue my sentence before Kaiden threw me over his shoulder and carried me until I managed to wiggle out of his grasp. I pushed his chest, which honestly didn't make any kind of difference.

"What the hell is wrong with you? You can't just show up and act like the hulk whenever a guy is involved!"

He hit the wall behind me, which sort of startled me, and those eyes pierced my soul. Those beautiful gray eyes that I wanted to stab at this moment. His face was inches from mine while his breath hit my cheeks.

"What the hell were you thinking when you agreed to go out with that dickhead? Oh wait, you weren't thinking, were you?"

I slapped his chest. "You are not my boyfriend! So, you don't get to tell me who I can or cannot see! And why the hell do you even care?"

Our voices were so loud it was echoing and once my last word stopped, it was quiet. A pregnant pause set in and in a quick motion my back was laying against the cold wall.

"I care about you. The last thing I want is for you to waste your time on someone like him who only wants one thing from you." He answered.

"Why do you even care? What possible reason other than your damn ego is there?"

"There isn't."

My heart fell. I was disappointed. I expected him to say something else. Something like he was jealous and that he didn't want me to go out with other guys because he loved me and wanted us to be together again. But maybe I was just imagining things the whole time, and he wasn't feeling the same way as I did. I couldn't read his mind, but one thing I know is that I didn't want to play these mind games anymore.

"You know, Kaiden, I seriously don't get you. You know what? It's really none of your business who I decide to go out with. So what if Caleb only wants one thing from me? Maybe that's what I want too. At the end of the day, I am single and you're my ex who has no say in what I do."

I walked past him, not even knowing where I was going, but just needed some space. When I got out of there, I saw the trees and the mist of the ocean from nearby that intoxicated me. I needed the fresh air. I needed to get out of his pride.

"You're not that kind of girl, Hailey."

I stopped in my tracks and the anger started coming out when I made my way back to him.

"You don't know who I am! You broke up with me! You left me. You went out and screwed different girls while I stayed behind, completely broken. So, you don't get to tell me who I am! Maybe it isn't me, but once again, that is none of your business! If you'll not do anything, then just leave me alone! I am going home because this is too much."

I don't know what his deal is with grabbing my arm, but he did it and we were now face to face. He softened up. Dammit, I was melting. My legs were jello and when we fight, it's somewhat exciting. I grabbed his jacket and pulled him closer to me, and once my lips made contact with his, the kiss intensified. He didn't hesitate to kiss me back, and before I knew it, he had backed me up against the fence, pinning my left hand with his. Our tongues danced around in each other's mouths and the taste of his minty toothpaste drove me insane. It was sometimes hard to stay mad at him. Especially after a kiss like this.

It was hunger and desire, all trapped in this heavy whirlwind. The moment he parted, I wanted to bring him back. Kaiden rested his head toward me, gasping for breath.

"God, you have no idea how much I've missed this. How much I missed you."

I pulled him back, and he trapped my bottom lip in between his teeth and destroyed any inch of space between us. His chest rose and fell with every breath he took. The closeness of our kiss set my whole body on fire. He asked me if I felt the same and with the way I attacked him, he should know. His hand fell, and I felt his warm touch reach under my dress, causing my body to tense as if he were touching me for the first time. At this point, everything around us had disappeared. I wanted him so bad at that moment. No, I needed him.

I deepened our kiss while his nails grasped my bare thigh, causing me to let out a moan. But with one squeeze, he released our kiss and grunted.

"I want you so fucking bad, Hailey, but I can't now and not here in this open place."

He took the joy out of what could have been a crazy ride. With the mess I had in my panties right now, I was so mad. He keeps leaving me so high and dry. I enjoy taking risks, but he kept in between the lines.

"C'mon, I am driving you home."

He went past me so fast, like he started regretting it all. I reached out my dress and adjusted my underwear because they were soaked. There was a lot that I realized as the months passed. It was that I liked the risk. It was exciting and for a moment, I would set aside my morals and just live in the moment. The tension in the car rose while we drove in silence for a short period. One thing I couldn't get out of my mind was how he knew where I was. The only person who knew was my sister, but they don't have any contact.

"So, how was your date?" He broke the silence.

"Is that just your curiosity, or are you genuinely concerned?"

You could see the smirk forming on the side of his face that the little of light showed.

"Both."

"Boring. I only agreed, so he'd get off my back about it. I'd rather play with a lion than have to deal with him alone for another minute."

He let out a roaring laugh, mocking me. Yeah, it wasn't my best judgment call, but honestly, it was hard not to laugh. He went on teasing me until he let out an uh-oh.

"What's going on?" I asked him.

The car pulled over to the side, and he was staring at me with embarrassment.

"So, I kind of ran out of gas." Kaiden said.

"How could you not have seen that you have any gas left?" I yelled at him.

"Well, you see what happened was I was going to get gas, but then I found out about your little date and then I completely forgot I needed gas. So, if you think about it, it was kind of your fault."

Kaiden tried to play it off as a joke, but to me it felt like he was gaslighting me once again. I tried to control the anger that was inside me, but I swallowed it and got out of the car.

"So, what are we going to do now, huh?"

"We're going to wait for Hunter to bring us some gas and just chill in the meantime."

Just great. We were in the middle of nowhere at this point, and now we are about to have who knows how long of awkward silence. I looked around and when I met his eyes, he was eyeing every inch of my body; basically salivating. Suddenly, I couldn't remain still and began to shift in my stop while he never took his eyes off me. The breeze hit me and now my skin was freezing.

"Are you cold?" He asked.

"Nope, just dancing. This is called the silver me timbers."

He let out a laugh before he took off his leather jacket and placed it around my shoulders. His scent was the first thing that got me and God, it was so good. There is no way I can focus on being cold with that just floating in my ever-waking soul.

"You're going to get cold, Kaiden."

He walked closer and wrapped his arms around my waist inside the jacket.

"Don't worry about me. I am warm enough now."

I could feel his smile on my shoulder like this was his plan all along. Such a charmer. My heart skipped a beat, and a smile spread across my face. He pulled me in tight and leaned against the car before I felt something that invaded our space.

"Is that—" I whispered.

"You don't realize how fucking hard it is when you're around, Hailey."

I looked up, and the hunger was back in his eyes, and the feeling between my legs had come back. I did something that you'd never expect. I moved from his grasp and opened up the backseat door.

"What are you doing?"

Like he didn't know. I climbed and relaxed on the seat.

"Come inside and find out. Or are you going to back out again?" I teased.

You could see that he was trying to fight every urge, but didn't win. He folded the moment he climbed in, closing the door and throwing me over his lap. My hands found their way into his hair and his tongue was dancing with mine. The bulge in his pants was rock hard and pushed against my hot core. He reached for the back of my dress and pulled the top down, exposing my bra. I propped my knees up and reached for his pants to unbutton, but I saw how he pulled back.

"Kaiden, I swear if you pull back one more time, I may actually explode."

He let out a laugh before reaching into his pocket and pulled his wallet to where he pulled out a condom. I was flooded with embarrassment.

"Just want to be ready, babe."

Kaiden unbuttoned his pants before pulling my head down, leaving a trail of his saliva on my neck and stopped at my breast, where he started sucking on it. I felt his hands reach under my dress and tried to pull my underwear off, which I had to get up a bit for that to happen.

"Fuck, you're so wet." Kaiden growled against my ear.

Feeling his fingers rub between my folds until they found my ever-needing bead that sent shocks throughout my entire body. His other hand found my bra latch and in a fast motion it was off, and now I was fully exposed. Forgetting everything in existence when his fingers entered me. I threw my head back while he kissed my neck.

"Ride them, baby." He demanded.

At this point, I lost all my sense while I swayed back and forth and his thumb evaded my clit, which drove me wild. I felt myself reaching my point, but with a thud, to the car, I jumped up.

"What was that?" I asked.

Kaiden looked over before letting a groan out. I pulled my dress up, covering my breasts while he had opened the door and right on the side of the car was Hunter, smoking a cigarette.

"How long have you been there?" Kaiden asked.

Hunter still faced forward, inhaling the cancer stick in his hands.

"For a few minutes. Are you done?"

This guy had some nerve, and I hid my face because I felt so ashamed. Hunter was someone you could not guess what he was thinking.

"Why didn't you say anything, for fuck's sake?" Kaiden sounded slightly annoyed.

I found my underwear and started putting them on, just forgetting my bra because at this point, who knew what he saw with these slightly tinted windows?

"I'd be an asshole not to let you finish. Don't stop on my account. Maybe you'll be less cranky, so have at it."

I looked at Kaiden, who was just rolling his eyes while I was completely mortified. He had buttoned his pants, and we both scrambled out of the car, but I refused to make any eye contact with Hunter. For him to not be bothered was shocking, but I guess they're best friends, so maybe this isn't the first time they found each other in this predicament. Great, now my mind was going somewhere it didn't want to again.

"Why don't you go warm up in my car while he refuels the take?"

Hunter gave me a grin and now I was flushed. He probably did see me naked. I felt chills running down my spine as I saw a glint of evil in his eyes.

"He's right. Go ahead and warm yourself in the meantime while I do this."

I hesitated, but nodded before making my way over to Hunter's car. I laid my head back on the passenger seat before I heard the driver's door open and Hunter hopping in. I saw him reach for the door and his eyes met mine and I heard the doors lock. My heart immediately raced as his face went from somber to intense.

"Good, we can finally have a little talk without Kaiden here."

A chilly breeze hit me and this car felt so small suddenly. I didn't like the way he was talking or even looking at me.

"T-talk about w-what?" My voice started to shake.

"Kaiden is nicer than I am. You saw something you shouldn't have seen the other night. And I just want to make sure we have an understanding that you won't be running your mouth to anyone, including the cops?"

I played with the sleeves on Kaiden's jacket and now I was having trouble breathing.

"I wasn't planning on it. I wouldn't do that to Kaiden."

My voice came off unsure because it was hard to talk right now.

"Good girl. Guess we won't have any problems. This went easier than I thought."

This was the first time where I felt really intimidated by Hunter to where I was shaking in my seat. Especially after knowing he was a dangerous criminal.

"What if it didn't?" The words slipped out of my mouth.

He thought for a second before returning his gaze to me.

"Just be glad it did."

The doors unlocked on cue and the door opened up, which caused me to jump. I found the handle really quick before zooming out of the car and made my way to Kaiden. The strange thing was his looks could kill, but even with being so damn dangerous, there was still something so alluring about him. I got into the car and was now looking at Kaiden's soft face. He gave me a smirk before taking off. I just wanted this day to end. We arrived at my house and he got out when I did.

"You look tired. You should get some sleep."

I smiled before wrapping my arms around his neck and kissed his cheek.

"Goodnight, Kaiden."

My lips lingered longer than they should, but it felt right and holding on is all I wanted to do.

"Wait, I have to tell you something before you go."

I put some space between us and waited for him to speak.

"Before I tell you, promise you won't freak out."

I nodded, mainly because I was panicking.

"It's about your sister."

My sister? What does she have to do with anything? They didn't talk, so what the hell did she do this time?

"Earlier today, I was helping her out, and she kissed me."

Shock, anger, confusion set in. She kissed him? My fifteen-year-old sister kissed the guy I fucking love? The feelings that were running through my bones weren't safe because I was angry. No, I was mad as hell!

Chapter 14

"What the hell did you just say?"

My promise went right down the drain. He held onto my arms, trying to calm me down, but there was nothing that could stop that.

"Just let me explain before you get all upset."

But there was nothing that could stop me. He started explaining, but the ringing noise in my head was louder and I kept hearing him say she kissed him over and over. I know he mentioned some creeps were following her and I should think about that first, but it was something else. He explained how she was having trouble at school and was getting bullied and that was what calmed me down. For someone who is always so headstrong, I never thought bullying would take her down.

"I took her back to my place when she explained everything and I guess she felt vulnerable and kissed me."

The protective sister came out of me.

"What the hell was my fifteen-year-old sister doing at your place, Kaiden? And why the hell didn't you tell me? You don't see anything wrong with this?" I shouted.

"I know it was wrong, but she was scared, and I didn't know what to do. She swore she would tell you, but I know it was best if it came from me instead. I pushed her off and took her right home."

I was speechless and furious at the same time. I didn't even know how to react properly to this. Should I cry or maybe scream and hit something because I was that angered? How could she do this to me? How could my own damn sister do this and try to justify it? I didn't give a fuck what she went through in school because, whatever it was, it still didn't give her a right to kiss Kaiden. To kiss the guy I've had a relationship with. The guy I shared kisses, and many other things with? I was so damn hurt and disgusted at this point that I had to stop myself from throwing up. I know Kaiden would never kiss her back, but that gut feeling just made things worse. I wasn't thinking straight at all right now.

"I gotta go."

I didn't say anything more, just walked right past him before going inside and straight to Alyssa's room. I shut her music off and slammed the door behind me.

"What the hell is wrong with you?" I yelled.

I saw red. Like I wanted to rip her hair out of her scalp.

"How the hell can you live with yourself thinking kissing Kaiden was okay? Are you that much of a brat that you have to ruin every good thing for me?"

My voice hit a whole different tone. I don't yell because it's not me, but this was the first time I've ever been pushed to an edge.

"W-what are you talking about?" But her stutter gave her away.

"You know exactly what I'm talking about! Don't you dare play dumb with me, Alyssa! Kaiden told me everything. How could you do that to me? What kind of sister does that?"

By now everyone in the damn block could hear me and I couldn't give two fucks about it!

"I don't give a damn what you've been going through in school. You can't blame it on that or use it as an excuse to be a shitty sister and kiss my ex!"

Guilt was on her face, but then it went neutral.

"What the hell did you think would happen when you kissed him, huh? Did you honestly think he was going to kiss you back? You're a damn minor and he would never in a million years touch you! And I can't see how anyone else would, for that matter. You are rotten and you're mean with no good qualities! No matter how much I try, you just have some kind of wicked vendetta against me, and I've had enough!"

Maybe I took things a tad far, but at this moment I didn't care. She has made it her mission to make me unhappy.

"You're lucky that I was raised better than you, because I would drag your ass in a heartbeat right now."

I was basically dry heaving, trying to catch my breath. My parents had stormed in at the right time.

"What in the world is going on?" My mom spoke up.

"You gave birth to the worst sister someone could ask for. She kissed Kaiden, Mom. Then wants to stand here and act like she did nothing wrong."

My mom was so taken aback and this brat still didn't say anything. No remorse either. Standing there looking like I was the one who was in the wrong. I could set a lot of things aside, but this was on another level of betrayal.

"Alyssa, is that true? Did you kiss Kaiden?"

All eyes were on her, but the way my father looked at her it terrified her the most. I think she hated it the most, but this is who she was. Always wanted to be the center of attention unless it was to hold her accountable for her actions.

"No, that's not true at all. He was actually the one who kissed me first."

Everything was rising when I went to snatch her, but my dad barely caught me in time.

"Are you that miserable that you would lie about something like that?" I screamed.

Everyone was conflicted, but I knew she was lying.

"That's a serious accusation. He can get in trouble, you know that, right?" My mom tried to reason with her, but knowing her, this is what she does. I couldn't believe her.

"This is what I was trying to tell you earlier. He really did kiss me first, Hailey."

She tried to give me such an innocent face, but I didn't believe it for a second. I tried to go get her again, but my parents didn't allow me.

"I don't believe you. You lie because your life is so pathetic. Go to fucking hell, Alyssa!"

"Okay, that's enough, let's go!" My dad said while dragging me out of the room.

He went back into the room and I hit her door. I was fuming, and this is it. I am never going to even try because she's sad. So fucking sad!

"Hey, what's going on?"

My brother came out of his room. I was not in the mood. I needed to get out of here quickly.

"She's a fucking psycho! She kissed Kaiden and is lying, saying that he's the one who did it!"

I didn't even hear what he said because I was already down the stairs, grabbing my keys. I don't know where I was going, but if I was in the same house as her for a second longer, I might have actually killed her. When I got inside my car, it struck me again that I had nowhere to go. So, I folded and decided to call Kaiden. This was about him and if there was any chance, she was telling the truth, then I needed to know.

"Hey, is everything okay?"

"Are you home right now?"

"No, I am at Hunter's. What's up?"

"Send me the address. I am coming over. I need to talk to you about something."

"What's going on?"

"Just send me the address."

I didn't let him continue to ask me more questions before I hung the phone up. I stared at my phone for a while until it lit up, showing he texted me. When the address came up, I clicked on it and made my way over there. It seemed longer than it truly was, but my mind went at a million miles per hour. Trying to grasp what was said tonight. I know Kaiden. I know his heart. He would never do that to me. Right? When I pulled into the driveway, I was shocked to see such a huge place. It's like Kaiden knew I was already there because he was outside smoking. I turned my car off and grabbed my keys and made my way over to him.

"Hey, beautiful. Twice in one night? Must really miss me."

I tried to smile, but I guess it came off that I wasn't in the mood.

"You look really sexy." He continued.

I could smell smoke mixed with alcohol and mint as Kaiden wrapped me in his arms. I wasn't here. My mind wanted to escape it all. Like the room was so big, and I was so small. Like a ringing noise is in my ear that's distracting me from reality.

"What's going on?" Concern appeared on his face.

I had to put some distance between us while I gathered what I was going to say. Part of me wanted to blame him. When I look into those gray eyes of his, it tells me they're only for me.

"I confronted my sister, and she turned it around saying it was you that kissed her."

Those eyes went huge. More shocked than I was.

"Is she out of her fucking mind? I would never do something like that! I hope you believe me."

I reached for his hand to comfort him. Of course, I believed him. I felt him calm under my hand but when he released it and walked away with his hand, messing his hair up. I knew he was mad.

"I believe you. Trust me, my sister has had it out for me for as long as I can remember."

Even my reassurance wasn't enough to fully calm him down.

"I knew there was no way that you could do that to me. I just got you back and I don't want to lose you again."

When I got closer to him, he was smiling at me. Now, this is what I love to see. I loved this man with every cell in my body. It was hard to explain the connection we carried to the unknown. There isn't anything that could stop that. Our bodies gravitated toward each other and trapped me in his kiss. Before I could inhale a breath, he backed me up until I was pinned against the rough wall. I tilted my head to look at him and saw a flicker of lust in his eyes. He went for my bare skin, which sent shocks of electricity down my spine.

"Fuck, I want you." He whispered.

I took a shaky breath and slowly nodded my head while feeling fingers caressing my inner thigh.

"Let's get out of here. I don't want to be around Hunter and his hoes while I make you scream my name."

My eyebrow raised and there was no doubt there wasn't going to be any more distractions. With the look on his face, he did not want to wait any longer. It was his need to be in control and my submission to him. Anytime I tried to take control, it never lasted long. One thing about him looking back on it now as I held a lot back. There were many things that I wanted to do, but they never fit into his plan. I know part of it had to do with the fact he never had any control growing up. Everything was not in his hands, but when it was with me, I let him have it. He was superior, and all I wanted was for him to love me and maybe, just maybe, he didn't need to fight for the upper hand. I wanted to be enough because a part of me thought he was way out of my league and no one as great as him could ever want me. I started realizing a lot and seeing different sides of him that he has never shown. I know I had a lot to do with that, but once again, my changing was not in his plans. But that's what you get when you love Kaiden Scott.

Chapter 15

When we arrived at Kaiden's place, he didn't waste any time kissing me intensely the second we got out of his car. Once we entered his house, he immediately grabbed me by the waist and pressed me roughly against the door. His hand was around my throat, taking the control he needed. It wasn't long before he picked me up by my ass and my legs on instinct wrapped around him. Never breaking contact while he carried me to his bedroom. My body hit the bed as he stared at me so hungrily. He pulled his shirt over his head and I could play that image in my head for the rest of my life if I wanted. He got closer, pulling the sweatshirt over my head, along with the dress from earlier. But once he had me fully naked, he just stared while licking his lips like he was just served that best damn steak. Even though he had already seen me naked many times, it never failed that I would get shy.

"I wish you could see yourself from my eyes. Because fuck, you're so damn sexy."

He climbed on top of me and our lips collided once again, our tongues wrestling for dominance, but he won. He always did. He grabbed hold of my hand and held it above my head as he gently bit the skin on my neck. If I wasn't horny before, then I truly was now. A trail of wet kisses left in the path as his head made it down to my panties, which were now wet again.

"I am going to taste you."

It was so low but loud and clear as he pushed my panties to the side and didn't waste any time. His tongue flicked slowly at my clit and my body crumbled on him. He stopped for a moment to pull my underwear off all the way before he got started again, but this time he went at full force and the shocks of my climax started climbing, but not before his fingers entered me at the same time. Pulling in and out of me until there was no holding back. My hands were now in his hair while I let out a loud scream and tried to pull back, but he held me down by pushing on my stomach. There was no escape from the sensation running through my body, but my legs shook as my orgasm struck. I felt myself pulling at his hair and now I was sensitive, but he kept going until I threw my head back again and cried out in pleasure. I stopped fighting it and rested myself to which Kaiden finally let up and wiped his mouth.

I laid there, catching my breath, when I heard a wrapper being opened and he was already naked while he was putting a condom on. He climbed back on me. I tried to move to get on top, but he held me down in place and wouldn't give me any control. I felt his tip at my entrance, just ready for it all. When he entered me, I let out a wince as his dick stretched out my walls until he was fully in me. A groan left his mouth.

"Fuck, you're so tight, baby."

Kaiden grabbed hold of my legs, instructing me to wrap them around him to which I did. Before he started slowing down, going in and out of me. He started kissing me again as his pace quickened and I felt every inch of him banging at my cervix. My moans were echoing throughout the room. Kaiden lifted himself up and put his hand around my neck as he pounded. I could tell he was already at his peak because, with one last hard thrust, I felt his dick convulsing inside me and he stayed in place, just pumping it all inside the condom. He had a long day, so I knew he was satisfied. I think I had teased him just too much. If I was honest, I hated condoms. I understand what they're for, but it would feel so much better without it. His hand released from my neck when he fell to the side of me, just breathing hard. I stayed there partially satisfied, but I knew I wanted more. Knowing him, he had always put everything in the first round that would probably knock him asleep. I waited a few minutes before I sat up and started searching for my clothes.

"You know, you could stay the night if you want."

I looked back as I was putting my underwear on and he had one arm, propping his head up to look at me.

"I need to get home before my parents call a search party. I did leave pretty upset."

The bed shifted before he hugged me and placed a kiss on my shoulder.

"That sucks, but I totally understand. Maybe some other night instead?" He asked me.

My head rested on his chest and I nodded. He moved my head over to his before he brought me back into a passionate kiss that would have me intoxicated. He reached over, pulling me onto his lap, giving me a little control.

"You're so damn perfect, Hailey." He whispered.

But that's the thing. I was far from perfect. That's who he wanted to see and what he always knew. I always jumped and did things that kept him satisfied. I was so blinded that I never knew the damage we were doing to each other. Like Bonnie and Clyde, but I realized that I wouldn't die for him. And when he realized that, I wasn't this perfect person he thought he knew. He started seeing me in a different light that wasn't so bright and shiny. Rather more work than he could deal with. The deeper we got into this, it felt like I was drowning. So, no matter what I did, it just wasn't enough. No matter how many times I tried, I found myself pulling further and further away like it didn't matter because it always felt like wrong timing. I just wanted to love him and I know he wanted the same. Life has a way of showing you signs you didn't think you needed until you realize it's too late. But I loved him.

Kaiden decided to take a shower before he took me to my car, which was still at Hunter's house. I was reluctant after my talk with him. He terrified me because I now know what he was capable of. I am sure if I had no relation to Kaiden, he would have killed me. He pulled into the driveway before turning his attention to me.

"By the way, Hunter is throwing a party tomorrow. Wanna come?"

With the way he threatened me, I wasn't sure it was such a good idea. However, if I told Kaiden he did that, then there is no doubt he would argue with him.

"It'll be fun. We will make an appearance and then maybe we could sneak away?"

Kaiden gave me his infamous puppy-dog eyes and I would fold. I smiled and agreed, but deep down, I knew it was a bad idea. They're best friends, so I need to try to get on his good side. He reached over and kissed my lips so gently before I made my way out of the car. Kaiden drove off already, but when I got to the car, it just occurred to me that I didn't have my keys on me. I checked my pockets over and over as if they would magically appear, but they didn't.

"Looking for these?"

I damn near peed my pants when I turned around and Hunter was standing there with my keys in his hands. My hand was resting on my chest while I captured my breath. I went to grab them, but he pulled his hand away.

"You know, Hailey, there's just one thing I am curious about."

Hunter played with my keys while looking at me and suddenly I felt a knot in my stomach. I could count the number of times we had any interaction on my hand. The last one wasn't a great one.

"What?" I said, trying to sound confident, but my voice said otherwise.

"You find out your boyfriend is a criminal and you just go with it. Why is that?" He asked.

He walked closer to me like he was trying to read my body expressions, or I honestly had no idea why. I took a step back until I was stopped by my car.

"You do crazy things for the people you love. I know Kaiden, and I know his heart to know he'd never do anything to hurt me."

Hunter stared at me for a bit before he started talking again.

"I guess that brings me to my real question. When will you drop this good girl facade?"

He let out a tiny condescending laugh, and it pissed me off, thinking he knows me. I went to reach for my keys again and again, but he wouldn't give them to me until he locked me into between his arms and his face was inches from me.

"I am not a bad person, and I could never be."

His minty breath was hitting my lips, and he didn't let up even a centimeter.

"I've met many people in my life to know when they aren't being their true selves. But Hailey, there's nothing wrong with being the bad guy. You'll realize how much better it feels to be feared rather than walked on. Anytime Kaiden comes, you tuck your tail between your legs."

His words just pissed me off.

"What is wrong with you? You think you could talk to me any way you want because what? You're part of a gang?" I yelled.

He laughed once again before he brought his lips to my ear.

"I'm not just part of a gang. I am the gang leader. Does that scare you?"

I swallowed roughly at his amusement while he backed away, giving us space. I was speechless, but I wasn't scared. I was angry. The thing was, I wasn't angry at him. I was angry at myself because I gathered the courage to tell him off, but instead, I kept my mouth shut. I let him talk to me that way, and all I did was stare at him angrily. He used my keys to unlock the car before he reached out to open the driver's door for me. I hesitantly sat in the seat before he bent down and handed me my keys.

"You may not realize, but I can see who you really are. This right here is a shell and I hate it because it's fake. Get home safe."

He backed away and closed the door and walked over to his house, where I saw a pair of female eyes staring at me. If looks could kill, I'd be toast right about now. In her eyes, I was a threat, but it wasn't intentional. I wasted no time driving out of there. I wanted to be as far as I could from Hunter Lockwood's house. He was right about one thing. That's how I am around Kaiden. He makes me nervous and maybe I've never seen his bad side because I tiptoed around it. He wouldn't hurt me, but it's so much easier if we aren't fighting. I wish I was more vigilant in my surroundings. I wish that could be me because if I knew then I'd know that we weren't alone, and the moment Kaiden came back to my life, everything just went downhill from there. How did I get myself into this mess? The one moment I stepped out of my comfort zone, it would change how everyone saw me. It would blow up in my face and I'd be forced to defend myself. *But the one person I least expected to count on was the only one there in the end.*

When I got home, everybody was already sleeping. And thank God for that, because I didn't want to face anyone. Especially not Alyssa. I was so wrapped in Kaiden that I almost forgot I was mad at her. I didn't want to have anything to do with her until she told the truth about what really happened at Kaiden's house. I didn't want to think about it anymore, so I went straight to bed until it was time for school. Which dragged on and, quite frankly, wanted to avoid Luna. I just brushed her off when she wanted information on what happened, but I wanted to keep it to myself. Why would I tell her when all she's going to do is give me shit about being with Kaiden? I wanted to be in my little bubble of happiness, knowing Kaiden and I were finally on a good path to be together again. I was happy. When night time came, I started getting ready for this party and I was quite nervous about going. Probably because Hunter will be there and he will look at me with those judgy eyes. When I was finished, I went downstairs to head out.

"Hey, Dad, I'm going out."

I reached for my purse, to which he stood in front of me.

"I don't think that's a good idea." He said.

"It's fine. I will be with Kaiden. You have nothing to worry about."

But apparently, that wasn't a good response either.

"I don't think you should hang out with him. Especially not after what happened with your sister and him."

My eyes shot up in shock.

"You can't seriously believe what she said. She's a liar and always has been for attention. You know what, this sounds more like another issue. But regardless, I am an adult and I'm going whether you like it or not, and you can't stop me."

I tried to walk, but he stood in front of me.

"I'm still your dad and you will watch the way you speak to me." He demanded.

"You just want a reason to hate Kaiden. You say he's no good for me, but at least he didn't make a bet to sleep with me."

Shock was an understatement. Because that's who he was in high school. He did that to my mom, but hey, they got a happy ending. I gave him another glare before I stormed out of the house. That was the first time I ever stepped out of line, but I'd had enough of people thinking they knew what was good for me. I've done pretty okay to make choices for myself that enough was enough.

Him and I

Chapter 16

I had arrived at the party and made my way inside and I knew absolutely no one there. Until my eyes met with those gray eyes that I love so much. He stared at me like I was the best thing in the world and the butterflies in my stomach started mutating. His eyes weren't the only ones on me. When I looked over, so were Hunter's who was next to him and my smile went away, while his smile formed. He knew he was under my skin and that was just his excitement of the night. Next to Hunter was the same girl from last night giving me dirty looks. She exchanged words with Hunter. I don't know what happened because not even a minute later, Kaiden had a guy pushed against the wall and he was mad as hell. I ran over to him, trying to figure out what was going on.

"Let me guess, that's your bitch?" That guy blurted out, trying to antagonize him.

Kaiden's hand went around the guy's neck and I was frozen. His temper was coming out. I looked at Hunter to see if he was going to react, but nope. He was just standing there calmly while taking a drag from his cigarette. He obviously didn't give a fuck about the situation, which I found a bit disturbing and I couldn't understand how anyone could be as cold as him, but I also wasn't surprised either. No one in the room was doing anything but watching it all go down. Why was I frozen? I wanted to do something, but I was a coward.

"That's enough, boys. We don't want any heads falling off. Do we?"

Everyone turned to the entrance, and this was the first time I had ever seen Hunter react. He was pissed, and so was Kaiden when he unlatched his hand from the guy's neck.

"How come I wasn't invited to your little party, brother?"

Brother?

Brother?

BROTHER!!!

There are more of him? I could feel chills crawl up my skin as the tension in the room started building up. They were exchanging words back and forth and at that moment I kind of wish I said no and stayed at home instead. I felt Kaiden grab me and pull me behind him as tons of guns were drawn out. I was so confused and scared at the same time. One thing that didn't make sense was why was Hunter so cold toward his own flesh and blood? Why was I the only one who didn't have a gun? I was drawing way too many conclusions and now I was lightheaded. They were talking back and forth, but the shock caused ringing in my ears and the only thing I could make out was Kaiden asking me if I was okay and that girl leaving. I buried my face against his chest, trying to calm myself down. My body was trembling like crazy, so he instantly wrapped his arms around me, making me feel so much calmer and protected.

"I'm sorry. This wasn't supposed to happen. I'm so fucking sorry, baby."

He was choked up on his words, and that made things really hard. I know this wasn't his intention, and it was out of his control. When I came out of the sudden shock, he had taken me upstairs to where it was quiet. He ran his hand through his hair, messing it up. He felt terrible and now I was the one comforting him.

"It's okay. You didn't know that this was going to happen."

I tried to reassure him.

"I brought you to a party full of criminals. I put you in danger, Hailey."

Kaiden had slid down from the wall and put his face in his hands. I walked over and bent down in front of him, putting my arms around his neck.

"You didn't mean to. It's okay. I'm okay. Please, let's just forget about it."

There was only one way to do that. I threw my leg over his lap until I was fully straddling him. At that moment, he looked up and knew exactly what I wanted. I crashed my lips on his and it wasn't long before his hands were squeezing my ass. I reached for his shirt and helped him take it off before our lips found their way to each other. How wasn't I the one scared and now I was comforting him? Was I doing this to make him feel better? This was my problem. I didn't want to be a burden, so I chose not to be the victim but the healer instead. I also didn't know that this was Hunter's room until he walked in.

"What the fuck, man?!"

I jumped out of Kaiden's lap and started fixing my dress because what else are you supposed to do in this situation?

"Ever heard of knocking?" Kaiden said.

"You're fucking me, right? You want me to knock on the door of my own room?"

Kaiden looked around, and I think he just realized it, too.

"If you didn't want me to enter, maybe you should've of lock the door before you start fucking. Or maybe choose one of the empty bedrooms in my house."

My cheeks were burning red at this point, and now both the men were laughing. We went to exit when Hunter had caught my arm to stop me from leaving.

"You're just proving my point. Who thinks about having sex after having a dozen guns pointed at her?"

He was smirking, which annoyed me. Why was he pushing so much? Like he wants me to flip out, or he gets off on being a dick. When we arrived back downstairs, everyone was being normal, like this was just something that happens on a daily basis. Hunter and Kaiden were drinking just having a hell of a time, and I felt so out-of-place like the black sheep of the party. This wasn't my scene, and it was obvious. I waited a bit longer to not feel rude, but there is only so much awkwardness someone can take.

"I need to leave soon. I have school in the morning."

"Alright, let me finish this, and I will walk you to your car." Kaiden said.

I just smiled and continued to stand there awkwardly until he finished, but then his phone rang and it just so happened to be convenient.

"Who is it?" I asked.

He shrugged before walking off to take the call. Now I was alone with Hunter and we had nothing to talk about. He just looked at me and kept drinking. I wish he would stop. He didn't even try to hide the fact that he was eyeing me up and down.

"You want one?" He asked.

I was completely lost in staring at all those tattoos on his body that I didn't really hear him.

"These are tattoos. Adults get those."

I rolled my eyes at his mockery.

"You're an asshole. You just find any chance to make fun of me, huh?"

He set his beer on a side table because he was amused.

"I offered you a beer, but then I remembered a good girl doesn't drink or smoke. I have second-hand embarrassment."

He reached for his beer and I just knocked it out of his hand and acted like it was an accident. I didn't know what came over me, but I had enough of his shit. Tonight has been exhausting as is.

"Sorry, my hands slipped."

But he wasn't mad. He was really amused. It was irritating.

"I do drink, but not on weekdays. Some of us actually go to school."

He crossed his arms and just stared at me with no expression.

"I can bet I am ten times smarter for someone who didn't finish school. Hey, Reed, pass me a beer, will you? Mine fell."

Some guy tossed him a fresh bottle, and he opened it with his teeth. Are you kidding me? What a show-off! He took a long drink.

"Let's not compare intelligence to incompetence. I'm sure you know everything about guns, but could you read the big words in the books, or do you need any help?"

He just laughed. There was no winning with this guy.

"A nerd asking me about big words. Now you're just boring me. I don't know how Kaiden could ever date a girl like you."

I was speechless, and he won because I was fuming.

"Excuse me?" I snapped.

But it came out more offended than I intended.

"You're so innocent. It's actually sickening. I could never date a girl like you. I'd probably end up corrupting you and you'll tell everyone I was the toxic one."

I was about to go in on him, but I felt Kaiden come back. When I turned around, it's like he had seen a ghost. He was red-eyed and just lost.

"What's the matter?" Hunter chimed in.

But he didn't say anything. He just stared blankly past us.

"Kaiden?"

I reached out and grabbed his arm.

"There was an accident, and my mom didn't make it."

Hunter and I exchanged looks, and the reading of the room was different. He was broken. The light in his eyes had shut out. His mom was everything to him. There was nothing anyone could do to help. Kaiden started unraveling and pushing everyone away. I wanted to take his pain away, but it wasn't possible. Do I hug him? Do I tell him everything is going to be okay? Because nothing is okay. Everything was a disaster. I walked over and wrapped my arms around him, but he didn't move. His arms lay dead at his sides. I was crying like I had a right to. I couldn't imagine what he was feeling. Kaiden's mom was a great woman. She treated me like her own daughter and she would even call me her daughter-in-law as a joke. But now she was gone. Life is so fragile, and it's scary to think that one day you're here and the next it could all disappear.

"I'm so sorry, man. I'm here if you need me." Hunter spoke up.

He didn't say anything back, which was understandable. I pulled back a little and now he was staring at the ground with a blank expression, fighting his tears off. But the thing about Kaiden is he holds a lot in. A part of him died that night with her. He felt like he failed her and somehow this was his fault, so he never let that go.

"I have to go. The hospital needs me to confirm her body."

He tried to walk off, but I stopped him.

"You can't drive in this state. I am taking you."

"Whatever, Hailey." He coldly said.

Looking back, I felt useless. I know I am making it about myself, but it's true. His mom died, and it changed him. It changed us in the long run and we never recovered. The Kaiden I knew wasn't who he was. We were so trapped in this wind of love that we never realized that's who we were. He had every right to act out the way he knew how to grieve. I could take it. I just wish he knew that he was allowed to feel. He was allowed to cry and be vulnerable. However, it was implemented in his head that it wasn't manly enough. So, I took the beating.

"I'm coming too. I'm gonna go and grab my keys."

Hunter went upstairs to where he got his keys and I think we had this unspoken understanding that we will set it all aside to be there for him. The ride to the hospital was quiet. When we arrived, Kaiden just got out without saying anything, but that's ok.

"I'm going to wait out here. I smell like alcohol." Hunter spoke up.

I nodded, but my feet weren't moving. It's the feeling of not being wanted there that stopped me.

"What are you doing? Go after him."

I took a deep breath before speaking. "Maybe it's not a good idea. He didn't talk to me on the drive here, so maybe that was a sign."

That annoyed Hunter even more. "For fuck's sake, Hailey. His mom died. This isn't about you. He needs you more than anything now. Now go be the good girlfriend and be there for him."

He was right. I made it about myself. I walked in and found Kaiden leaning against the wall, just silently falling apart. It seemed like he wanted to scream out, but he didn't allow himself to. I walked over to him and nuzzled his shoulder, but I knew he didn't even notice I was there. It's selfish to say, but I hope I never have to go through this. My parents mean everything to me, but the fact was that she was the parent he loved more. I know for a fact he would choose his dad to die if he had a choice. He'd be sad, but he wouldn't be torn up. My eyes stayed on the ground, just avoiding eye contact. Suddenly, his body tensed and pushed it off the wall.

"What the fuck is she doing here?" He yelled.

I looked in the direction he was looking at, and that's when I noticed his dad was there and he brought his girlfriend. Kaiden was unpredictable at this moment, and I was kind of scared. Charlotte was hugging William like they had lost her. Kaiden stormed over, but I managed to be the divider between them.

"I don't want that lying gold-digging bitch here, and you have some fucking nerve bringing her here. That is my mom! She is nothing to you."

He tried to push through me, but I barely was able to stop him.

"We're in a hospital, for Christ's sake. Calm down." William's tone was unbothered.

"Calm down? You want me to calm down! You're the reason my mom hit rock bottom and now you bring this whore here to insult her! Where the fuck do you get off!"

His voice echoed the halls and anyone in the hall just so happened to tune in to the family drama.

"I was the one who insisted on coming with him. Your father wanted to come by himself." Charlotte spoke up.

"Shut the fuck up. I wasn't talking to you." He yelled.

He was right. She shouldn't be here. His mom's heart broke when he divorced her, and this was wrong. For her to speak up like she was some saint was one thing, but to act like she did nothing wrong was another.

"That's enough. Don't talk to her like that. What is wrong with you?"

I can promise you that there was no stopping him. I moved beside Kaiden and held on to his arm.

"I'll talk to her the way I want. This bitch is the reason Mom drank herself to death. You choose someone half your age over Mom. And she's dead because of you! Now, you're dead to me, which doesn't matter because you believed this whore over me. So don't you dare talk to me like I am the problem."

The tears were finally breaking out, because he wanted to do this all along. He never got a chance to tell his father how he really felt, so this was his breaking point. Kaiden felt like he had nothing to lose, so he let it all out.

"Enough! I know you're hurting, but you can't blame us for your mother's death. She had a drinking problem way before our divorce."

The tension in the room became too much and if I didn't step in, then he would hit him.

"Kaiden, let's cool down for a second." I said.

But he snapped. "Stay out of this, Hailey. Actually, I don't even know why you're here. Just go home. I don't want you here."

I looked at him, shocked. He would never talk to me like this, yet he did. In my head, I just kept saying he was acting out, so he gets a pass. His mom died, so him treating me this way was okay. Right? I was too stunned, so I just stared at him in disbelief.

"I said go home! What part of that don't you understand? Do I need to fucking spell it out for you?"

His words made me want to die. I think he realized he was a tad too harsh because he walked away before saying any more. My eyes started burning as the tears were coming out. It didn't matter how fast I blinked, they were there. But my feelings didn't matter, so I let it go.

"You have to excuse him, Hailey. He's not himself right now. I do think it's best if you go home, though. I'm sure he'll call you when he's calmed down."

His hands interlaced with Charlotte's as they walked away too. Now I was standing there with a hallway of people looking at me. But I couldn't do anything but take the beating so that I didn't overstep. Because grief is one thing, and Kaiden didn't know how to handle it all. It was so much for his heart to take that he forgot he wasn't alone. I know I didn't have a right to cry, but when someone you love talks to you like trash or like they weren't just kissing you passionately not long ago. Kills you. I smoothed out my dress before making a brief exit, and as soon as I was outside, the tears were on full blast. It took a minute or so but Hunter came into eyesight and if I didn't know any better, then he seemed concerned.

"Hailey? Why are you back already? Where is Kaiden?"

But I resorted to ugly-crying, and that freaked him out. He kept asking me questions, but I couldn't think straight to give him an answer. You could see the panic. Yet, he did something that was least expected. I felt a pair of arms wrap around me and when I looked up, it was dark skin and that confirmed it was Hunter. Hunter fucking Lockwood was hugging me. If I wasn't a mess, I'd take a picture because there is no way I would think he would pity me in any way. But I took advantage of it and clung to his shirt. Do you know what it's like to meet someone who doesn't expect anything from you? That he does things for you and not because he would get something out of it? That's who Hunter was. But he'd deny it if you asked him. Who would've thought that the most feared man in L.A. would be the most loyal to a few and even me?

Such a turn of events, but I was grateful he put his pride down to show some kindness. He didn't say anything until I settled down.

"Let me drive you to your car."

I nodded as I retreated to the passenger side and endured another quiet car ride. When he pulled in front of it, he got out to walk me to the door.

"I know I don't deserve your kindness, but thank you."

He still remained with his neutral expression before nodding and turning away to go back to his vehicle.

"Wait."

He stopped walking and looked back at me. He gave me a gesture that was telling me he was waiting for me to speak. I mean, I didn't stop him from leaving for no reason.

"Why are you being nice to me all of a sudden? Usually, it's all teasing and insults from you."

He sucked on his cheek and he gave me a cold stare now.

"I'm doing this because of Kaiden. Otherwise, I wouldn't give two fucks that you're crying. I'm a criminal, Hailey. Nothing about me is nice. So don't think for a second that's going to be our new thing."

But his eyes said something different from what he was saying. I used to say that reading him was impossible, but honestly, he wasn't that hard to figure out when you got to know him. Each person carries different demons and the way that you're brought up just shapes you into the person you are. I was fortunate, and that made me ashamed. I couldn't relate to pain the way that they could. I couldn't do anything but watch it all play out because I had the perfect parents with the perfect family. I was Ms. Perfect. But what was perfect? I didn't have anything together. If anything, everything just kept crashing down until I broke. So, when I did break, it caused everyone around me to question me as a person. Hunter walked back to his car, and I stood there until he left and just took a moment to breathe. This day was just horrible, and I needed it to end.

Chapter 17

When I woke up the next day, I wasn't feeling it, but I knew after school I wanted to go check up on Kaiden. Maybe he needed some space, and that's fine, but it didn't hide the knot in my stomach. I wasn't in the mood to get dressed up or to put make up on either. I could barely even focus on school right now. I kept staring at my phone, hoping he would text and call, but let's be honest, he was preoccupied. But you can bet that when school ended, I was already in my car headed to his house. He needed me and I was going to be there for him, no matter the abuse he gave me. I mean, he would do the same for me, right? Hunter's car was parked outside, so I was happy that he wasn't alone. The door opened up when I came to the front house and there was my "best friend".

"What are you doing here?" He asked.

"To see you. Why else would I be here?" The sarcasm rolled off my tongue.

"He doesn't want to see anyone at the moment."

My eyes met the back of my head like he thought that would stop me. It was so easy for him to change personalities, but this one thing that isn't negotiable.

"Yeah, well, try to stop me. I am not leaving."

I brushed past him and headed to Kaiden's room, which I was sure he was in. When I opened the door, sure enough, there he was, half in the bottle. From the red eyes and the darkness under them, you can tell he hadn't slept, and he was drunk. But when he saw me, all it showed was disgust. I gave him my cute smile, but his demeanor didn't change.

"What are you doing here?"

"I came to check on you since you're not taking my calls or text."

He threw back the rest of his beer before walking over to the mini-fridge and taking another one out.

"Yeah, because I've been ignoring them. But the straight-A student apparently can't take a hint."

That hurt. But it wasn't about me, so I took the beating. He's hurt, so he's pushing me away.

"How are you feeling?"

That question seemed to piss him off even more.

"What kind of stupid question is that? My mom died and you're asking me how I'm feeling?"

That's where the last foot dropped.

"I was just asking. You don't have to be so rude. I've done nothing to deserve this." I argued.

"You think that's rude? I always knew you were a damn prude if you can't take that."

I walked over to him and grabbed the beer out of his hand and put it down on the bar table. This was going too far, and it was not him.

"You're being a jackass. You have every right to act out, but to treat me like this is not okay."

He picked up the bottle again and took a long sip, and his cold-hearted attitude was on full display. It's funny because I wish I could say that this was the only time. Eventually, I stopped making excuses for his behavior.

"I thought chicks like jerks?"

That voice in my head was telling me to leave, but the stubborn part of me thought I could make him have a breakthrough. It's silly thinking about all the things that lead up to where I am now. So, taking the high road is what I tried to do. I walked over to him and started rubbing his arm.

"Kaiden, please, this is not you. Let me be there for you."

"If you want sex, just say that. No need to butter me up."

Done. I was done. It was not worth it. I headed for the door before he caught my hand.

"Wait. I'm sorry. I just. . . I don't know how to deal with this, okay? Please don't leave me."

I melted like butter. My tail tucked between my legs and I caved. I was still angry, but I agreed. What kind of girlfriend? Friend. Would I be if I said no? I wanted to yell at myself to go home and not skip school, but that's what I did to be there for him. He calmed down and didn't treat me horribly for the next week when I went to visit him after school. He wasn't fully himself, which pained me seeing him like that, but he had a good reason. I was just happy he wasn't calling me stupid or a burden anymore. He allowed me to be there and take care of him, even if we weren't talking. Until the day of the funeral. I wasn't expecting anything out of him. I was going to sit there and be quiet. For the memorial, I sat in a different row to give him the space he needed and didn't seem to want too, anyway. But it was real, seeing her in that casket. The air was thick and there were flowers everywhere. Flowers are supposed to be full of excitement, yet they are filled with sorrow and pain. Kaiden didn't shed one tear, while everyone was flooding the place with tears. I wanted so badly to hug him and make everything better. Hunter, Kaiden, and I stayed back when everyone left, and it began to rain.

After minutes of silence, Kaiden began to raise his voice and stomp his foot out of frustration. Cursing the world for taking his mother. But nothing could be done to make it any bit better. He let out a scream before taking his sunglasses off so now you could see he was fully crying.

"I can't do this." He tossed his glasses to the ground and took off.

I took off after him, calling his name, but he ignored me each time until we got to the parking lot.

"Can you please stop walking for just a moment?"

When he finally did, I was catching my breath.

"What is it, Hailey?"

"Look, I know you're hurting and there is nothing I can possibly do to make this better. But we can get through this together. Please stop pushing me away."

He hit the hood on his car that left a dent before turning to me with anger. Full rage.

"No, Hailey. I won't get through this. How can I ever get through losing the most important woman of my life?"

I made my way over to him, taking the hand he used to his card and pulling it to my heart.

"It won't be easy, but we will, together. Just one step at a time. Like you said before, it's you and I against the world."

I felt like I was trying to plead my case, but his grief saw nothing.

"I can't. I have to leave."

He fumbled with the keys in his hands to open his car.

"Go where?" I asked.

The silence between the time I asked and his answer seemed like a decade.

"I don't know. Somewhere far away from here. From this town. I'm leaving."

He turned around to open his car, but I walked over and turned him back around.

"The hell you are. You can't run away because that won't help you. I won't let you leave."

I was so drenched in the water that I was barely about to say a word without spitting a mouthful of water. He wanted to leave and at that moment, I would have done anything to keep him there. He fought for me and I wanted to do the same for him.

"What about us?" I selfishly asked.

He lingered again, but the cold expression on his face spoke a million words.

"For fuck's sake! There is no us, Hailey. Now just leave me the hell alone!"

It wasn't the last time he would treat me so horribly. He wasn't thinking, but he made it personal. He wanted someone to blame, so he blamed me. He used me as his own personal punching bag. The tears were piling up and the pain set in that he was doing this to me again.

"That's not what you said a few days ago. You promised! You fucking promised!" I yelled.

"Yeah, well, what I said. Forget about it. From now on, you can do whatever the hell you want. You're leaving for New York in a few months, so this is just getting a head start. Goodbye."

The entire world was breaking down, and I was falling apart. Like I was going crazy. He got into his car, but I walked to the window and hit it.

"You promised! You lied! You're a liar! You promised!" I cried out.

But he started his car and drove off and my legs buckled under me and I was sitting in a pile of water, falling apart. He has broken me not once but twice and I barely recovered from the last one. He walked away broken with no care in the world and threw us away like it was so easy. After everything we've been through. After getting me to fall for him again. He left behind promises that he couldn't even keep. I couldn't explain it, but something broke inside me again. Being the nice girl never got me anywhere but walked over and dismissed me. I was so over it. I swore to myself that day, I would never allow anyone to fool me like that again. Kaiden Scott was my world, but I wouldn't die for him anymore.

"Come on, you're all wet."

I looked up to see Hunter standing there with his hand out and without a fight, I took it and just followed him. I was numb and there weren't any more tears left to cry. Hunter took me back to his house to get dried up. I don't understand why he is hot and cold but it's expected of him, I guess. He left me alone in a bar and usually I wouldn't but this time I thought fuck it. What did I have to prove to anyone? I reached back and got a bottle of scotch. I poured a shot and took it back, not before choking on it but, whatever. I poured another one and threw it back when Hunter came back in.

"I don't have any clothes for you, but you can borrow a shirt if you need one. Wow, slow down there."

I just gave him a look before taking another shot.

"You know, you're right about one thing. Being the good guy sucks. You give and you give and people just take advantage of you. So you know what, I am just going to drink my sorrows away."

I grabbed another shot glass and filled them both up with tequila.

"Maybe you should slow down. I am sure you don't have a high tolerance or such."

He walked over and took the other shot from me and threw it back. I felt the tears coming on again and just thinking of why I was acting like this. Why am I even here in the first place? I get it, Kaiden wasn't himself, but you would think after everything he would just ask for space. Not just throw me away.

"Jesus, can you stop crying? Here, drink it away, because I can't stand your tears."

The cold-hearted Hunter appeared, but what did I have to lose? I am tired of people treating me anyway they want because I allow it. I allow others to walk over me, and I always apologize for their wrongdoing.

"I am hurting, you asshole. Have a little compassion, will you?"

He went back to his beer and just gave me a look like "do you know who I am". I took a seat on the barstool before grabbing the bottle and deciding "fuck it". I opened the cap and started drinking from the bottle.

"And you think Kaiden isn't hurting? He lost his damn mother and you're making this about yourself? Never knew the innocent Hailey could be so selfish."

I took another sip before slamming it down.

"You know what Hunter? If me having feelings is selfish, then I guess I am. I spent the last week being called dumb, easy, replaceable. I put up with it and allowed it to get left once again. Like I was nothing. I get that he's hurting, but it's not an excuse to allow him to treat me any way he wants. It's toxic. So you can save me the name-calling. I've had enough for a lifetime!"

What was weird was that he let up and wasn't so stiff anymore. He took another drink from his beer and let out an "ahhh" after.

"Let him grieve in peace. He will come back to you when he's ready. Trust me, that boy loves you for whatever reason."

However, I wasn't sure if I'd allow him back. I'd forgive him because he wasn't himself. However, I couldn't forget how he talked to me and how inadequate he made me feel. I guess it was just too soon to tell. With the back-to-back shots I took, I was already feeling it. But I was nowhere close to being done already. I had filled the shot glasses up again and Hunter gave me a look. I held it up, waiting for him to cheer me until he did and that was another one.

"I won't be able to go home until I sober up. So, you're kind of stuck with me."

For the first time, he gave me a smile because, well, I am drunk. He was so used to seeing me closed off and shy that this was rare. So, he enjoyed the carefree Hailey. He made it so easy to let loose and not to care. Because I can promise you if my friends, family, and Kaiden saw how I was acting now, they would disapprove and try to bring me down to my senses. Like I needed to be fixed, but that wasn't what I needed, nor did I want to. To think about it, that's what I came to admire about Hunter. He didn't care what others thought, and he didn't try to change anyone's opinions about him. He embraced it. While I am labeled the good girl but when I said something died in me when Kaiden left. I meant it. But it was for the better and it showed everyone's true intentions and my trust wasn't something easy to have. Nor was it easy to get back because there were boundaries that were set.

"That's fine. I will take you back when you're sober. I guess I can babysit until then."

I gave him a dirty look, but that infamous smile was back that he was trying to hide behind the rim of his beer. So let's embrace this moment. Where, for once, everyone in this room wasn't anyone but themselves.

"Then you need to get on my level, at least."

I poured him another shot and again he gave me that "what the fuck" look, but I used the whole I am bad boy against him. He had trouble with this one, but he took it back and he made me forget why I was getting drunk in the first place. But the consequences of drinking so much were catching up to me. I think that last shot got him because we were laughing and just talking and before we knew it, hours rolled by. If you were to tell me days ago that Hunter and I would be sitting here, getting drunk together and having a good time, I'd tell you that you're out of your mind. Now I see why Kaiden cherished him because he owed me nothing, but has done more for me in a matter of days than anyone has done for me in years.

When the laughing died down and we were both past our limit, we stared at each other quietly. Who knew all along this was all I needed from anyone? It was a damn gang leader, but he wasn't all that I made up in my head. He was normal with a twist of insane. He finished the tiny bit of his beer and set it down before reverting his attention back to me.

"So. . . here's the issue. I was supposed to drive you home, but now I am not able to do so. I can call you a cab or you can sleep it off in my guest room because we're both wasted."

I looked at Hunter and my vision was clear. He was leaning on the counter, trying to keep his balance. I lied because my vision was anything but clear.

"If I go home this way, my parents will have a conundrum. Sleep doesn't seem so bad right now."

I stood up and could barely keep my balance, so he grabbed my arm to keep me up. He was just laughing at me. Drunk Hunter is fun. I know this may never happen again, but it's a nice memory that I would keep for the rest of my life.

"Alright. I will help you to my room to change and then to the guest room. I wouldn't trust you on the stairs. You may scratch them." He ordered.

His hand laid on the middle of my back as I stumbled to his room and it felt like it took hours, but I did it. Barely making it in and finding the closet, I chose the first thing that was there and started stripping.

"Wow, usually people wait till the room is empty before stripping."

Hunter turned around while I got dressed.

"Thank you for being so nice to me. You can turn around now." I spoke.

I sat down on his bed while he turned back around to nod at me. All excitement and letting loose was dying down because I knew tomorrow, I had to face reality. The reality was that Kaiden left me and my heart was broken.

"You got me drunk, so I don't know if I should be grateful. But let me show you to the guest room."

I went to stand up, and I lost my balance, but not before Hunter had caught me. As a reflex, I had grabbed hold of his neck and we both fell onto the bed and he was on top of me. It was all the emotions at once and the mix of the alcohol and I think we both were a little hazy because he didn't move. He stared at me, all glossy-eyed. I don't know what happened, but his lips were on mine and I was confused. I know we were drunk, but I knew exactly what was happening. I caved in to his kiss and it was getting hot and heavy when he repositioned himself and his hand was holding my head. I think he finally realized when he rolled off me and now was holding his head lying next to me. I was just as shocked because I touched my lips and, well, I know I said that Kaiden was the best kiss I ever had, but it was nothing compared to this one. How was this possible?

"Fuck, I'm sorry, Hailey. I shouldn't have done that. I am not in the right mindset."

His eyes were closed and his hands were still on his head. I turned to my side to get a better view of him. I felt my lips again, and I wasn't thinking about anything or anyone. I wanted him to kiss me again.

"Hunter. . . " I whispered.

He looked over at me and the expression on his face told me he wanted the same thing. I moved my head closer to his and brought him back into another kiss. This time it was slow, but the passion was everything.

"I can't do this. We're drunk and then there's Kaiden. . . ."

He leaned his forehead against mine, but his hand was still holding the back of my head. Was it the liquor courage or was it the way he was looking at me? Like he sees me. How could something so wrong feel so right?

The words came out before I could stop them. "I don't want you to stop."

He struggled with his inner voice, which was lost. But he wasn't still convinced yet.

"Hunter, I want you."

That was the confirmation he needed because I didn't even finish speaking when he pulled us back into a drunk, passionate kiss that will stay on my lips for the rest of my life. Like it was tattooed on my skin and nothing would ever compare to this. This was the moment that changed everything. Like the script was flipped and now I was at war with my heart. His hands wrapped around my body like it were made to be there. Even for a drunken decision, it stays implemented in my brain and I'd have flashbacks trying to justify this. But the way his tongue invaded my mouth, our bodies moving in sync, and how he let me have all control. I was fully intoxicated now, and the timing was horrible, but nothing prepared us for the morning after I had sex with Hunter.

Chapter 18

When I woke up, all I could feel was the pounding in my head and the moonlight beaming through the curtains that burned my eyes. My mouth was dry and when I tried to sit up, the room was spinning around me. It took me a few minutes to realize why I felt this way. I looked around the room and immediately recognized it wasn't mine. A cold breeze hit my skin and when I looked down. I didn't have any clothes on. There was a warm body beside me and then it was clear as day. His arm was around my waist and Hunter was naked as well. Then I remembered. We had sex. I went through all stages of grief, denial, remorse. Glimpses of the last night started playing in my head. Especially when I told him I wanted him. Guilt struck when Kaiden came to my mind and I was so confused at that moment and didn't know what to think. My intense headache and the shock made it difficult to piece everything together. Like the fact I was the bad influence for making him get drunk with me. I basically jumped out of bed when I felt the sickness in my stomach and I was vomiting in Hunter's toilet.

I basically threw up every content of my stomach until I was dry heaving. I managed to lift myself up, but it was a struggle. I turned the water on and splashed my face with cold water, hoping that would help. Drying my face with a cloth, I looked in the mirror to try to see how bad I looked, and that's when I saw Hunter standing in the doorway.

"You alright?"

Shame washed over as I tried to cover my naked body like he hadn't already seen me naked. He walked over until we were inches apart and we made eye contact like he was sorry, but not sorry about what happened. His arm extended to grab the towel hanging and handed it to me, but his eyes were fixed on my face. He wrapped me in the towel and the embarrassment broke my gaze at him. His hands at my chest closing the towel but he never stopped staring as if he was trying to read my body language. But the way his face fell meant the guilt was coming to him. We betrayed Kaiden in the worst way one could ever possibly betray someone they love and care about. What was I thinking about getting us both drunk? To sleep with his best friend? I am the worst person ever.

"What have we done, Hunter? Kaiden will never forgive us when he finds out about this."

I began to panic and words started coming out, not even making a complete sentence. Just shock.

"Can you calm the fuck down?"

But I couldn't. I was sick with guilt and everything was a mess now. It's my fault and now I have to live with knowing I betrayed the man that I love.

"Calm down? You expect me to calm down?" I blurted out.

"Yes, calm the fuck down. What happened between us was a drunken mistake. So, it stays between us because I would never in a million years sleep with you if I was sober."

That hurt. No, that was fucking painful. Not like it mattered, and I won't show him he hurt my feelings.

"You think I would if I was sober? I love Kaiden, and I would never do something like this to him. I would never even sleep with an asshole like you."

I was trying to convince myself more than anything, but his expression didn't change and the heartless Hunter was back. Maybe it triggered him more than I expected, as he tensed up.

"Yeah, well, you already did, but hey, this asshole brought you back to his house after your ex left you crying in the rain. But hey, I am the bad guy, right? Because you can't take any responsibility. You were the one who got me drunk. You told me you wanted me and it's my fault?"

He was really triggered.

"I could easily give zero fucks, but the way he left you. Somewhere deep down, I actually pitied you. Which never happens. But again, I am the asshole."

Ouch again. I felt like the asshole now. He was right. I mean, he could be very mean and all. That was definitely not a lie, but that day, he was kind to me in his own way. I think this whole situation made me act a certain way and say things I didn't really mean because, deep down; I knew it was my fault. I wanted to apologize to him, but it felt like my mouth was taped shut and I couldn't open it. Instead, I just stayed silent and avoided his gaze. He didn't deserve this after he was so nice to me.

"Now listen to me carefully, we'll pretend nothing ever happened. Alright?"

But that's the thing. I couldn't pretend it didn't happen.

"Are you saying Kaiden isn't going to know what happened? You can't expect me to keep this from him."

"I am not asking, Hailey. This will go to the grave because I won't let this mistake ruin my friendship with him."

He was dead serious too. His whole demeanor changed, but deep down he was scared. Kaiden and he were so close that it would be like losing a brother.

"But this will eat me alive. I can't lie."

Hunter hit the counter that got my intention.

"Dammit, Hailey! I don't care. You won't say a word. You're going to keep your pretty mouth shut and forget this happened. Believe me when I tell you that you will keep this a secret because you don't know the things I'd do for the people I care about, and you don't want any problems with me."

He walked closer to me, trying to intimidate me.

"I am not just any criminal. I own this city and I am feared across the globe. So, keep your fucking mouth shut."

My heart started to pound and I felt chills down my spine as Hunter got closer and trapped me between the sink and him. Not only did I sleep with Kaiden's best friend but also with the leader of a dangerous gang.

"I'm not going to hurt you. Just want to know if we're on the same page."

I couldn't speak, so I just slowly nodded. He backed away and I finally let the breath I was holding in.

"I mean, we don't want to hurt Kaiden, right? Especially now. If he knew, he would want anything to do with you, so it's what's best."

He took my silence as co-operation and Hunter's lips curled into a satisfied smile before he walked away and left the bathroom. I suddenly felt a lump in my throat that was suffocating me, and on top of that, my head was pounding like never before. This was the part where I said that I would never be drinking again. I felt the vomit coming up again. When I finally got the courage to leave, Hunter was on his phone sitting on the bed. I didn't want to speak to him, so I walked over to the bed where my clothes were and basically darted out of the room, slamming the door behind me. I slipped on the clothes from last night and I was feeling like crap, and Hunter wasn't doing anything to make it better. He changes his attitude so quickly and I don't know how he could do that. I held in my tears when they were about to come pouring out. I went down to the bar to collect my phone that I had left there and it was dying. Looking at the aftermath of our drinking party. Sadness took over me just knowing the shitty person I was. This wasn't me.

"What's wrong with you?" Hunter interrupted my thoughts.

"Are you seriously asking me that? Everything is wrong. I feel like the worst person in the entire world because I slept with Kaiden's best friend. I feel like shit."

Now I was crying again. Flashes of our moment together came spiraling to my mind. Because no matter how shitty I felt, I didn't regret it. *When I accepted to go further, he asked again, and I said yes. A different side had come out while I got on top of him and he pulled me further until I was holding the bed frame. Licking my clit until every inch of my body was shaking and screaming out his name. The way he had me in that same position as he slammed his dick in and out of me while his hands were in my hair.*

I came back to reality and Hunter was giving me a soft look while I reminisced last night.

"I'm sorry. I don't know what else to say to make you feel better. I'm not exactly the type of guy-"

"To give a fuck about these things, I know. It's fine, Hunter. I don't blame you. If anything, it's my fault and I only have myself to blame for making that decision."

I grabbed my purse and made my way past him.

"That's not true, and you know it. It takes two to tango, so it's not just your fault. The damage is already done and we can't undo it. Now let's just forget about the whole thing. I mean, it was just drunk meaningless sex, right?"

I guess he regretted it, but nothing about the way he kissed me was meaningless. I don't regret him. I just regret hurting Kaiden when he already is going through so much. That's where being selfish got me. But I won't give him that satisfaction.

"I have to go." It was all I could say.

He's only the second guy I had ever slept with, so why would it mean anything to me? I walked past him, but he still wouldn't let me go.

"Let me get showered first and I will take you home. I'm not a complete asshole." He teased me.

Great, now I felt like shit again. Hunter drove me home in silence after he got ready and dropped me off a few blocks from my house so no one would suspect anything. There was no use in talking because I had to try to forget all of this. His eyes stayed on me until he saw I was close to my place before driving off. But my brother was out front when I got there.

"What are you doing here? I thought you'd be with Kaiden?" He asked.

"No. Kaiden left town. I am going to go inside and take a shower and then sleep."

I tried to skip all this talk, but he wouldn't let up.

"He left town? Wow! But why do you smell of alcohol? That doesn't seem like you."

See what I mean.

"Listen, I've had an awful night. I just want to go to sleep."

But I was crying again, and that caused my brother to wrap me in his arms and I just fell apart. Kaiden leaving and me sleeping with Hunter reminded me that staying in my bubble kept me safe.

"What's wrong?" He asked.

I cried louder, thinking about it.

"I did something terrible." I cried out.

"What could you have possibly done that was so bad?"

I waited a few minutes before I finally said it. I needed to tell someone I trust.

"I slept with Hunter."

He held me in his arms while I told him everything and it didn't take any weight off my shoulders, either. He didn't agree with me about keeping it from Kaiden, but I didn't really have a choice. Hunter unintentionally, but intentionally, threatened me at the same time. I also wanted to forget this nightmare, even when it's going to haunt me for a long time. Brandon managed to calm me down and sneak me into the house without my dad or uncles noticing me. I stayed in the shower, trying to scrub my sins away. What was I going to do? This changed everything, but even if I wanted to tell Kaiden, he was long gone. I tried to sleep but couldn't bring myself to do it. I just kept finding myself crying until there weren't any tears left.

My sister had come into my room and she was the last person I wanted to see.

"Are you ok?"

"I'm fine. What the hell are you doing in my room? Get out!"

I turned back to the window, but she didn't leave.

"I saw you crying, so I know that not everything is fine. Did something happen between you and Kaiden?"

She couldn't be serious.

"You're delusional if you think I would tell you anything after what you did. Get out of my room and leave me the hell alone. You can't be the villain and try to be the savior at the same time. It doesn't work that way!"

Not everyone has good intentions and everyone around me proved that. Because faces become strangers and strangers become something you know so well. There's a reason you don't keep secrets, because life has a way of showing you why you don't. People find out. I was dumb enough to think I could keep this forever. I was mad that I didn't tell him myself. For the next week, I just ignored everyone and went to school, then came home and slept. Like I was in this loop of sadness. Kaiden didn't reach out, and I knew he wasn't coming back. I tried to call and text him, but he switched his phone off. I was worried. The clock showed it was ten at night and once again, I couldn't sleep. What was I expecting? I know I should be forgetting all this, but it was insulting to text Kaiden at the same time. But one thing he said stuck in my head. I am leaving for New York in a few months so we would've broken up anyways. Imagine if I would've stayed just to be in a place where my heart gets broken twice? My phone started to vibrate, which was weird. I nearly fell off my bed when I saw who it was from. I looked at the message that said "come outside".

I didn't even think twice before I ran out and he was leaning on his car with guilt written on his face. Was this a sick dream, or was he really here?

"Kaiden, what are you doing here? I thought you left town."

I kept my distance just in case this was another sick mind trick. He was staring at his hands and shame was written on them.

"Actually..."

He took a deep breath before standing up and walking over to me.

"I never left, Hailey."

HE

NEVER

LEFT!

This made things ten times worse because now he was in front of me and I had this secret that could send him off the edge. Like the icing on the cake. I didn't know what to do, and I was terrified. Kaiden took a few steps closer to me, and now he was within an arm's reach. His face was bruised and now I was shocked. What the hell did he get into?

"What happened to your face?"

I reached up to touch it, but he caught my hand mid-air.

"It's a long story, but I'm fine. I can tell you all about it at my place. If you have nothing to do right now."

I hesitated mainly because I was guilty, but because the way he talked to me a week ago and stood in front of me being sweet just didn't make any sense. I just nodded and walked to the passenger side without saying anything further. The drive there was quiet, but it didn't stop me from looking over and seeing the look on his face. Like he was battling with his inner thoughts. When he pulled into the driveway, we both walked into his place, but I stayed close to the door just in case this gets worse and I need to leave.

"Want something to drink?"

I shook my head no as he put his arm out, telling me to take a seat. I hesitated, but I walked over and sat down and he sat next to me. He stayed looking at me and no words were being said.

"Are you going to tell me or just keep staring at me?"

That came out ruder than I wanted, but whatever.

"Sorry, it's just that I have missed seeing your beautiful face."

I don't know, but that angered me. He switches his emotions like crazy and I just don't know how he was able to drop me so easily and then come back again like nothing ever happened. Hell! I was acting that way too. We were both on edge, but mine was from guilt.

"I never left town, as you can tell. I got in my car and I started driving until I got to Hollywood and realized I didn't even know where to go." Kaiden explained.

"So, you're telling me you've been in L.A. this whole time?"

He just gave me a nod. But there was something so calming about how he was acting. He was being himself, but it was only sadness. I couldn't believe this and now I felt sick to my stomach. To find out that Kaiden has been here this entire time, and I slept with Hunter. I couldn't even make eye contact because I was ashamed. I was sweating and almost shaking.

"Hales, are you okay?"

Truth be told. Nope. I was far from okay.

"I- I need some air."

I ran out of the room and out the back of his house, which was on a hill. This can't be happening. None of this should have happened. If I only knew, I sure as hell would not be drunk and I wouldn't have made the decision of sleeping with Hunter. I am not blaming him for my actions, but this could've been avoided. I heard Kaiden walking behind me.

"Hailey, I'm sorry. I should've told you right away. But I just needed to breathe."

I turned to face him and he was sincere. But only one thing made me question it

"Did Hunter know about this?"

Chapter 19

If Hunter knew before we had sex, I will raise hell and Kaiden hesitating made it all worse.

"He did the next day. Which is why my face looks like this. He came to pick me up."

Great. Just fucking great. If what I did wasn't enough, he had to get beaten up too?

"You see, after I left the church's parking lot. I didn't know where to go, so I stopped at a bar in Hollywood and had a couple of beers. I was pretty buzzed, so I went outside and just started walking, not caring where I ended up, which was a dumb idea because I went to a bad part of town and happened to run into a rival gang. My dumbass decided to antagonize them, but they brought my mom up and everything was foggy after I took the first punch. But I was outnumbered and got my ass knocked out. I didn't wake until around midnight. I was pretty fucked up, so I had to call him."

I guess this explains why Hunter insisted on keeping it a secret. He knew that it would blow up in our faces if he were here. I went over and shoved Kaiden.

"How come you didn't call me? I would've been there for you. Kaiden! You could've been seriously hurt, and you just ran off without telling anyone. How could you be so damn selfish? I spent the last week worrying about you and was heartbroken, yet you can't even give me the courtesy of sending a text?"

Ironic, huh?

"Because I didn't want you to see me like that, Hailey. You would've freaked out!"

"Yeah, I am freaking out now!" I yelled back.

"Believe me when I say this, but it was for the best because I've been a total mess this whole week."

He was doing it again. This had nothing to do with Hunter anymore. Because this has been a long time, coming that I finally stood up for myself.

"I had time to think, and I realized I couldn't do this on my own. I need you, Hailey."

Old Hailey would've caved and said that this was okay. She would've hugged him and forgave him, but that's not what I deserved.

"You left me, Kaiden. You called me stupid and made me feel cheap. You broke your promises and basically said this was a long time coming since I was leaving. No, you're going to stand here and say you need me? You broke me again! I went insane after you left me crying like a fool in the rain. I let you in after you said you wouldn't do that again. You need me? I NEEDED YOU!"

Did I even have a right to speak like this? Were my feelings even valid?

"I obviously didn't mean anything I said. I was hurt and wasn't thinking clearly. I didn't mean to hurt you or play with your feelings the way I did. It wasn't my intention because I would never hurt you on purpose, Hailey."

I know he meant it, but there was that gut feeling that said I needed to speak my mind.

"And what happens the next time something tragic happens, huh? Will you keep belittling me and abandoning me? If that's what I am in for, then I don't want it. I have feelings too and I sent them aside to be there for you. I can forgive you, but I can't forget the things you said to me."

His face fell, and he was scratching the back of his head now. He felt guilty. I felt guilty.

"I'm sorry, Hales. I know that doesn't make up for the things that I've said. But you're the only good thing in my life and I need you."

I wrapped my arms around him because I wanted to put this all behind us now. He needs me and I will be there for him. He had a long road to healing, and that's all that matters. But now, I couldn't be mad at him for acting the way he did, and for wanting to be alone. He lost his mother, and he acted out. No need for me to make him feel like shit anymore. He didn't mean it, is what I kept telling myself. However, I do wish that things had happened differently because then none of this would've happened in the first place. Like me sleeping with Hunter. I will forever feel like crap. I love him and that's all that mattered.

"Hailey?"

"Yeah?" I replied.

"I really don't want to be alone tonight. Can you stay with me?"

I exhaled heavily hearing the pain in his voice and even if it wasn't a good idea. How could I say no to him?

"Of course."

His arms wrapped around my tiny frame, and that was the hug he needed. Oh! Kaiden. Where did it all go wrong? We didn't stay up much longer, but he held me close all night until he was sound asleep. It felt weird and not the same anymore. When morning came, I woke to the sound of Hunter's voice and my adrenaline was at full speed.

"Yo, Kaiden. You awake?"

He walked into the bedroom and I avoided eye contact because how do I explain this to him?

"What the hell, man? It's early!" Kaiden screamed out.

He had slowly gotten out of bed and so did I, but the tension was so heavy in the room. Hunter looked at me and I was suddenly shaking in my skin. There was no normal after that. I hadn't seen him since we slept together, so it was awkward. With the way we were both acting, I was surprised Kaiden didn't catch on.

"I'm going to have a quick shower. You both keep each other entertained in the meantime."

I grabbed his arm, not wanting him to leave, but he just smiled and walked away. Great, just freaking great. Hunter gave me one last look before walking out so I could get changed. I knew once I did then I had to face Hunter, which was the last thing I wanted. Last time we were alone, we had Jose and Jack and got naked! I took a moment before coming out of the room and went downstairs. He was looking at his phone and as soon as I stood in front of him, he didn't pay any mind to me. Until I coughed at him.

"Want to take a picture, or do you still have the image of me in your mind?" He teased me.

I shoved him. How is he so nonchalant about this? How could he act like nothing happened? I know this is what we agreed to, or more like I was threatened to do, but I couldn't just act normal.

"How come you didn't mention what happened to Kaiden? Or tell me that he never even left town?"

He just looked at me like I was the crazy one and, to be honest, I felt like the crazy one. This was eating me alive, but it wouldn't change anything either because what's done is done.

"I don't have your number, so how the fuck did you expect me to tell you?"

"You could've messaged me on Instagram or Facebook or something!"

Hunter started laughing like there was a joke.

"You're fucking kidding me, right? Do you really think I have any of that crap?"

He went back to laughing, and I wanted to punch him. I swear if I didn't know his age, he would act like he was forty and give me life lessons.

"Why do you have an Insta account, then?" I asked him.

"And how do you know I have an Insta account?"

Then it hit me. Now he knows I've creeped on his account. But this was back when he slept with Luna and she would obsessively search on his account and then gush when he posted new pictures, but I was guilty hoping he'd post one with Kaiden during the time we were broken up.

"Has the good girl been stalking me?"

Hunter smirked at me with his arms crossed against his chest, waiting for an answer.

"Ewww no! What reason would I have to stalk you? I mean, it's not like you post anything but you in a car. But really, who gets to take pictures of you? I don't understand."

Hunter started laughing since I was already caught. Might as well make fun of him.

"I can't help it. The ladies love me in my car. You've seen it, right?"

Yup. He wins. He got me to shut up with that one.

"You know. . . If only you had stayed a few more hours at my place that day, you would've known as soon as he called."

Is he serious?

"Stayed a few more hours? What possibly would I have done there after my initial freak out?"

His hands started rubbing his 5 o'clock shadow, but he already knew the answer and just kept me waiting.

"A few more rounds." He whispered.

I threw my hand to cover his mouth.

"That's not funny, Hunter. Speak a little louder! I am sure the neighbors didn't hear you!"

He moved my hand off a bit.

"We had—" He tried to speak.

However, I covered his mouth again.

"I am going to kill you if you keep it up."

Yet my threat wasn't enough. I removed myself and put some distance between us, but he was just laughing. Not before he took a brief exit with no words. It amazed me how mysterious he was and I hope to God Kaiden wasn't around to hear any of this. For someone who wants to forget, it happened, he sure as hell wanted to talk about it the most.

"Where are you going?" I yelled.

"To smoke. You're more than welcome to join if you want."

"I'd rather take first-class to hell than join you!"

But I could never win.

"That would be my bedroom! Have you been there?"

I stomped my foot in frustration. He is so annoying, but I still remember how we were before we had sex. Now he laughed and actually talked. The way he is now was more words than he said to me before Kaiden and I broke up the first time. But with what we did, we both got a first-class ticket to hell. I waited there for Kaiden to get out of the shower and when he did the way, he walked over to me with a smile, knowing not even five minutes ago he would have heard everything.

"Where's Hunter?" He questioned.

"Outside, torturing some innocent birds."

Kaiden laughed, but he winced a bit when his smile came. His face looked like crap. I walked over and placed my hand on his cheek, slowly rubbing the large gash from when he hit the concrete. He placed his hand over mine.

"It feels better than it looks." He tried to reassure me.

I didn't believe him, but I know he was trying to make me feel better.

"I can't stop thinking about what those guys did to you. I could hardly sleep last night because seeing all those cuts and bruises was haunting."

He took my hand from his face and placed a kiss on my knuckles.

"They could've killed you. Kaiden, I don't know what I'd do if I ever lost you. Just being without you for an hour drove me insane."

His hands rested on my hips as he brought me closer to him.

"Yeah, but they didn't. It's going to take more than a few cuts and bruises to get rid of me, Hailey. I'm okay."

But selfish Hailey was coming out. I wasn't thinking at all. And the problem with me is I never think before I act. Because if I ever stood there and thought about something clearly. None of this would've happened. The words that came out of my mouth got me in trouble.

"You didn't deserve this. Maybe you should stop hanging out with Hunter as much."

He pulled back a little to look at me to see if I was serious.

"What? What are you talking about?"

"He's going to get you killed, and it's kinda his fault that those guys hurt you."

Why was I saying this? A part of me was thinking this was a way that I never had to see Hunter again. I mean, it's not like Kaiden would listen to me regardless. Hunter is a criminal, but he wasn't an awful guy. At least not to me. I need to think before I react, but I had already said it even though he wasn't having it.

"That's not true, Hailey. It's not like it was Hunter's men who beat me up. Trust me, my mouth was the reason I was attacked. Let's just let it go."

He was smoothing out the loose hairs that were on my cheeks. He comforted me and I knew the old Kaiden was back. But I couldn't let it go.

"Hunter probably has tons of enemies, and you being friends with him can be dangerous, Kaiden. The next time, they could seriously injure you. I worry."

"I've been friends with him since we were kids, and nothing has ever happened to me. I am not going to drop my best friend because my mouth got my ass beaten up. Stop worrying."

One would think I'd let it go, but I kept going. Even with that voice inside my head kept telling me to shut up because what would this solve?

"I know this life gives you adrenaline, but I don't want you to be a part of it. It's dangerous, and it's not you, Kaiden."

Kaiden just smiled and placed a kiss on my forehead.

"I love how caring you are. But it's okay."

My back pocket suddenly vibrated, and I reached for my phone and saw that I had a new DM on Instagram. I backed away to see it was a message request. It was Hunter.

Hunter: Come to the front door.
Hailey: What? Why?
Hunter: Because I fucking said so.
Hailey: Excuse me?
Hunter: Can you for once just do what I say?
Hailey: How do you expect me to go to the front door while Kaiden is here? Are you insane or what?
Hunter: I don't care if you say you're in labor, just hurry up! Or else I'll tell him about what happened between us.

I was fuming, yet did what I was told.

"It's my dad. I gotta call him. I will be right back."

I made my way to the front door, where Hunter was standing. He was pissed. I closed the door behind me and he was internally killing me right now.

"What the hell is your problem?" I tried to keep my voice down.

He slowly walked toward me until my back hit the front door.

"My problem? You're asking what the fuck my problem is? Tell me what yours is?"

I looked at him, confused. I had no idea what he was talking about.

"I honestly don't know what you're on about." I rolled my eyes.

He slammed his hand next to me, making me jump.

"I overheard what you said to Kaiden. What are you trying to do, huh?"

Fear struck me, and now I saw why everyone was scared of him. My breathing became hitched, but there was no denying this.

"I—"

"You what?"

His face was inches from mine and he walked closer to the point where I tried to take a step back, but my head hit the door.

"You want to call me an asshole, go ahead. You want to say I am cold and dangerous, fine, whatever. But what you're not going to do is talk shit and try to sabotage my friendship with Kaiden just because you couldn't keep your clothes on!"

I thought Kaiden being an asshole was bad, but this was a whole other level.

"You don't see me trying to ruin your relationship, which I can do in a heartbeat. I have nothing to lose." He silently yelled.

"I wasn't trying to—"

"Don't give me that bullshit. I know exactly what you were doing. Try that shit again, Hailey, and I will show you exactly why I am not the good guy."

I pushed him away from me. I was tired of people speaking to me like I won't say anything back.

"I am trying to protect him! This is your fault!" I screamed.

"Protect him from what?" He asked.

"FROM YOU! I am trying to protect him from you and your bad decisions. You want to be a gang leader. Okay, fine. But Kaiden is getting hurt just for knowing you. Nothing good comes from getting involved with you!"

This wasn't like me. I don't yell or get angry like this, but this is what Hunter does. He finds your weak points and brings the worst out of people. In me.

"You want to protect him from me?" He let out a snarky laugh. "Hailey, Hailey. Naive fucking Hailey. You know damn well that's not the reason you don't want him around me."

He leaned forward until he was right next to my ear. "You don't want him around me because you're afraid he'll find out his name is not the only name you've screamed. Am I right?"

I once again shoved him off me. "You son of a bitch!"

"Oh me? What? I had you in every fucking position begging for more and I am the issue? Yeah, he needs protecting from me. I am not stupid, nor am I oblivious to the real issue."

I went in to slap him, but he caught my hand in mid-air.

"I love when you get aggressive. It turns me on. Just like when you rode my tongue, and your moans echoed the whole fucking house. I stopped seeing you as an innocent girl the moment you put my dick in your mouth."

A cocky smirk formed on his lips as his eyes roamed over my body.

"I liked the wild side of you. Plus, you tasted fucking delicious too. You know what?" He rubbed his chin with his hand. "I've changed my mind. Let's tell Kaiden what happened between us right now. Then I can take you back to my place and fuck your sorrows away. Again."

I was so taken aback I couldn't even speak.

"Wh-a-a-t?" I muttered out.

"You heard me. Let's go tell him."

My chest was going up and down as my breath started to increase. He changed his attitude, and I wasn't ready.

"Tell me what?" Kaiden spoke up.

I was so stunned no one heard him coming out the front door since we moved away from it. My eyes were big. Kaiden's were curious and Hunter was smirking away like he was the king of the fucking world.

"Hailey has this covered. I have to run and go do bad boy things. You kids have fun."

He walked off, leaving a large elephant between Kaiden and me. How was I going to explain this? Do I tell him? Hunter is a coward for walking away like that. He turned back and smiled at me sadistically before vanishing. The worst part was I just got a glimpse of who Hunter is, but I could very well see that was just the inch of it. I will never get used to it. Ever.

"What was that all about?" Kaiden asked.

Chapter 20

I picked at my nail buds and was shaking, trying to come up with what to say. Maybe I should tell him the truth. "I. . . I. . ."

It wouldn't come out. I had the opportunity, and I blew it. Like why did I carry this weight on me when I could've been honest. But the thought of losing him at the time was worse. I didn't want to lose him and I didn't want him to stare at me as his enemy when he would find out.

"Well? Come on, I can handle it. Rip it off like a band-aid."

But I still couldn't speak. He was being so nice and understood that I panicked. I can't destroy him. He already lost his mom and if I told him the truth, he would lose his best friend and me. I was a liar. Kaiden started to look at me suspiciously, so I had no choice but to lie.

"Well, you weren't the only one drinking after the funeral."

I resorted to half the truth.

"Don't tell me I was the reason you were drinking?"

I took a deep breath, replaying the fight in my head. Screaming at that, he promised.

"You hurt my feelings that day, Kaiden. Something inside me broke. Especially when you said *there's no us.* So yeah, I drowned my sorrows away. Hunter actually drove me to calm down at his house, and I took advantage of his full bar. Sort of made him drink with me, but he basically babysat me."

Kaiden threw his head back in shame and he was blaming himself, which was the last thing I wanted. That was my problem.

"Forgive me for being a shitty kinda boyfriend."

I walked over and pulled him into a hug.

"Already forgiven."

***

Hunter

What a goddamn mess this whole thing was! There weren't a lot of things I felt bad for, but the one thing that was killing me was betraying my best friend. So, I hid it with sarcasm and jokes, but the moment I heard Hailey try to fuck up our friendship, I fucking lost it. Until I saw the fear in her eyes. I didn't like that she feared me, but when her fear turned to anger, I knew she was about to exit her comfort zone. From the moment I met her, I knew under that good girl exterior was someone who can fight and hold her own.

"Hailey has this covered. I have to run and go do bad boy things. You kids have fun." I said before walking out the door.

I watched as she was freaking out, but it was fun watching her squirm. She wasn't going to tell him, but I know she was fighting that voice in her head on doing the right thing. I pulled my keys out of my pocket to go to my car, but I heard a rustle coming from the side of the house. I reached to the back of my pants where my gun was at and quietly went to check what it was. When I got closer, there was a man watching Kaiden and Hailey. What's worse is that he probably heard what we were talking about. I snuck behind and he didn't hear me before drawing my gun and whacking the back of his head. The guy fell down, and I placed my gun in his face.

"You better have a good fucking reason before I paint these bushes with your blood!"

He looked at me terrified, so I knew he wasn't gang-affiliated.

"Who are you?" I yelled.

"I—" He stuttered.

It pissed me off more, so I pistol whipped his ass again and now he was bleeding from the back of his head to the side of his cheek. He was in shock and could hardly speak. I noticed he was carrying a small backpack, and that was even more suspicious.

"What's in the bag, huh?"

Yet he stayed frozen.

"Start talking before your mom has to plan your funeral."

"Alright, I'll tell you. Please don't kill me." The guy pleaded.

"I am a private investigator and I was hired to spy on the guy that lives here. The bag has pictures of things I've seen so far."

I grabbed the bag out of his hand, but still aimed the gun at his head. "Who the fuck hired you?"

When the barrel of the gun touched his head, he caved. Fucking coward, didn't even put much of a fight. "Luna Moore."

Luna? Luna! Why the fuck does she need to know about Kaiden? I grabbed the guy by his arm and dragged him over to my car.

"Are you going to kill me?" He asked with tears forming in his eyes.

"Not yet."

I hit his temple with the handle of my gun and he was out cold. I shoved him into the back of the car before making my way inside. If Luna knows shit and with how fucking dick-whopped she is, something needed to be done. I worked too damn hard not to have everything taken from me. But the root of all issues is Hailey. Luna is her damn best friend. I walked back inside and there she was. Laughing and acting all innocent with Kaiden, like her nails weren't scratching my back a week ago. She was far from it and it drove me mad. I know if Kaiden ever found out, he would try to say it was me who took advantage of her because she's just not that person. If only he knew what the innocent Hailey was capable of.

"We need to talk." I finally spoke up.

Hailey's eyes went to my gun, and she went into puppy-dog mode while Kaiden went into hero mode and pulled her behind him like she needed it.

"Why the hell is your gun out, man?"

I don't think I rolled my eyes this hard before.

"Because I am going on a fucking picnic. Stop asking dumb questions and hurry up. I don't have time for twenty questions."

If only people would do as I say, I wouldn't have to get annoyed so fast. If I have my gun out, that means shit is about to go down. Idiots, I swear.

"Alright, fine. Let's go somewhere before you give Hailey a heart attack."

He didn't notice, but I did when Hailey gave him a look. She was tired of being looked at like every little thing scares her. It startled her, but she knew what to expect from me. Kaiden walked out of the room and her eyes looked at me like the villain again.

"Must be exhausting being in character all the time." I said.

She gave me her famous face. "Bite me."

I let out a laugh because I love fucking with her. She gets mad and her nose scrunches up, and it's fucking adorable.

"I already did, remember?"

Her cheeks turned a bright red, and she knew and that's all that mattered. I walked past her, but she quickly grabbed my arm.

"Wait, you're not going to tell him about. . .?"

Her finger gestures back and forth between her and I. Why does she make things so easy?

"Oh, tell him about how far your legs—"

She cupped her hand over my mouth again, and I couldn't help but laugh some more. Getting under her skin was just too easy and I enjoy that.

"Why are you doing this to me? Torturing me?" She asked me.

I didn't really have a good answer for that, other than I enjoy it. She should know I wouldn't risk my friendship over a quick fuck. But she is so paranoid and lets me get to her.

"You're easy to piss off and I'm bored. Kinda hot when you look like you want to hit me. Now, if you don't mind, I have more important things to deal with than your paranoia."

I walked away and met Kaiden in the common room, and I almost forgot the reason I asked him there.

"What took you so long?" he asked.

"Never mind that. I have something important to show you."

I grabbed the bag that the guy had and pulled the photocopies out, and then I tossed them on the coffee table. Kaiden looked over, stunned.

"Oh, that's just some of it."

I handed him the camera where he was able to see everything else.

"Apparently, you have fans. There was a P.I. taking pictures and videos outside your house and I caught him. Apparently, Luna has it out for you. She hired him."

He tossed the camera on the couch and his face was turning red.

"Where the fuck is this guy?"

I couldn't hide my smile. He's about to see my handy work.

"I knocked his ass out, and now he is taking a nap in my car. Go get rid of Hailey so we can find out what's going on."

He let out a sigh of frustration and pinched the brim of his nose.

"Alright, I will take her home and we will deal with this."

He started walking toward the kitchen, but stopped for a second and walked back. Oh fuck. Here comes the drama.

"I have a bone to pick with you. You failed to mention you took Hailey to your place and got drunk with her."

Fuck. She is good. Real good. I left her in an awkward space, and now I am getting scolded. Alright, she wins. Kind of proud of her, and I deserved that. I hid my smile, thinking about it.

"You should've taken her straight home. What the hell were you thinking? Hailey can't handle her alcohol, let alone being sad too."

This idiot needs a wake-up call.

"I promise you. Hailey is a big girl. She said she didn't want to go home after you humiliated her, so I was just being nice. If anything, I'm the victim here. She got me drunk, not the other way around. Maybe you should give her a lecture about forcing tequila shots down my throat."

He was not amused, but I sure as hell was.

"It's not a joke, Hunter! Hailey isn't like us, and that could've ended very badly."

Badly? Quite the opposite. I had a great time, and so did she. But unfortunately, he can't know any of that.

"You should be thanking me that I babysat her after she was ugly-crying in a puddle. You know I have better things to do than to take care of her emotional ass. You should blame yourself, not me. Anyways, hurry up."

His daggers were painful because I just gaslighted the hell out of him because what I did was worse than what he did. I went to exit the room, but he stopped me this time.

"Where did you take her afterward, though? Because there is no way she would go home drunk."

Fuck. I didn't even know how to answer that one.

"Are you guys done talking?"

Saved by Hailey. For once, she came at the right time. Well, she came a lot. But in this situation, it's different. I need to get my head out of the gutter. Kaiden's phone started ringing, and he left the room.

"You were eavesdropping, weren't you?" I asked her.

But she was annoyed again. I wonder if this is how she is with Kaiden too, because she's already becoming a pain in my ass.

"Doesn't matter because you should be happy that I did. I saved your ass, so I'd suggest being nicer to me."

So fucking adorable. I got closer to her while she was trying to be the tough girl.

"No, sweetheart. You saved your own ass because you know you'd lose your sweet, precious Kaiden. You had your chance to tell him the truth, yet you didn't. How come? I thought you wanted to be honest?"

Her walls dropped, and she tucked her tail between her legs.

"I know what it is. You want to keep the best night of your life to yourself and not share it with anyone, huh?"

Her lips curled and I couldn't help but laugh. One day, she is going to fully snap and I hope I am there to see her do it. A force to be reckoned with, and I am here for it.

"I do want to tell him. I just don't know how."

Hailey let out a sigh and dropped her head down. I almost felt bad, but those were just excuses.

"This is what you say. Ready? I had sex with Hunter. Easy as hell, right?"

I looked at her and gave her a smirk that she melted into. Like she was annoyed but intrigued at the same time. She had nothing left to say, so I made my exit. That's the thing about me. I've had tougher conversations. Here's the thing, though. If the truth were to come out, yeah, I'd be hurt, but I'll recover. Someone like Hailey won't. Watching her fall apart after Kaiden left was kind of sad. Which is why I took pity on her. If she were any other female, I would have left her there no matter the situation. But there is something about Hailey that makes me soft. It was wrong, but I was ready for the consequences.

Later that day, I made my way over to the spot the P.I. said he and Luna were meeting. I was really hoping he was lying, but as soon as I saw the blonde hair, I fucking knew. I snuck up behind her and wrapped one of my hands around her throat while my other hand held the gun to her head.

"Make a sound and I will kill you."

She stayed still and started panicking.

"We're going for a ride, and no, you don't have a choice."

I grabbed her arm and dragged her to the car and made her get inside before returning to the driver's side. When she finally gets a good view of me and the fact that she knows what I am now. You can see all the scenarios playing in her head. I wasn't in a murderous mood, but I can be if things go south.

"W-Wh-ere are we going?" She stuttered.

"Did you know that I like long walks on the beach? I even brought my best beach toy."

I started laughing, but that only worried her. I thought it was a funny but tough crowd. I pulled up to the parking lot before instructing her out of the car.

"You've been a very bad girl, Luna. And bad girls get punished. Sadly for you, you won't like this."

I grabbed her arm and forced her to the area where Kaiden and one of my gang members were waiting. When she saw her precious P.I. she knew. Her eyes went to Kaiden and back to me. I was just curious as to why she was spying. I knew she was obsessed with me, but this was a different level of insane.

"Oh, my God!" She screamed.

This was me. This is how I handle things and honestly, I didn't enjoy it, but it got my point across. Her hands were shaking and the sweat beads were rolling down her forehead.

"We know everything, and it's time to start talking." I whispered.

She was looking all around like she was going to find an escape, but there wasn't any.

"I'd suggest you start explaining, because I can't understand why you would hire a spy to stalk me." Kaiden went on.

She was not responding, but shaking in her shoes. This shit was really getting irritating and minutes had gone by. I lifted the barrel of the gun until it touched her head.

"I'd hurry if I were you because I am getting impatient here."

Luna began to sob annoyingly.

"I only hired him because Caleb forced me to. He wanted to find things to show Hailey so that she'd leave you and he could be with her. I didn't want to, but he was blackmailing me. I swear, I was flipping the script, and I wasn't even going to tell him what I saw."

Someone as shallow as she was hard to believe. However, she isn't dangerous, just naive.

"You lie a lot. How do I know you're being honest?" Kaiden asked her.

"I swear! Hailey's my best friend and I wouldn't do anything to hurt her."

That was probably the only thing I believe, but what a fucking shit show. Everything happening is because of Hailey. She was just some girl and yet she has managed to cause everyone to do stupid things. It's fucking Hailey Davis, and she caused me to do something so stupid. My mind drifted to that day.

"I want you."

Those three words sent me into overdrive. The way that it came out of her mouth and some would say it was her rebounding, but that's not what it felt like. I never knew the obsession with her until I saw her. I saw the real her. It was almost intriguing, but irritating at the same time. I snapped back, forgetting what we were doing in the first place.

"No! I didn't show him anything. You have to believe me!" She cried out.

Here's the thing, though. This guy knew things and the last thing I needed was loose ends.

"Someone has to pay."

I moved my aim to the P.I. and without hesitation fired. The bullet went through his chest and he fell to the ground, gasping for air before all life went out of his eyes.

"Why did you have to kill him?" She cried out.

"He knew too much, and pretty boy wouldn't allow me to kill Hailey's best friend. But if you weren't, I wouldn't even think twice about doing it. But just so you know, I never give second chances. So, keep your mouth shut and we won't have any issues. Now get the fuck out of my sight."

Luna didn't think twice before darting off in tears. Kaiden looked at me with relief, but part of me wanted to do it. But Hailey-fucking-Davis was the reason I was doing things I wouldn't do.

***

Hailey

I woke up to my phone vibrating and when I looked at my alarm clock, it was midnight. No one ever calls me this late unless it's Kaiden. Worry started filling me, so I was quick to answer.

"Is everything okay?" I immediately asked.

"Can you come over? I need to see you."

There was something different in his voice. I've heard that before, but this time there wasn't any emotion behind it. I was scared he was going through a mean sprout again, and that worried me.

"It's a school night, Kaiden. I can't just go right now."

It was that gut feeling that told me not to go, but this was Kaiden. I would've done anything for him.

"Just come."

Something was wrong, so I agreed. Yet when I agreed, the phone call ended. This was strange and I wish I would've listened to the gut feeling. I quickly threw on some clothes and plotted how I was going to sneak out without getting caught. I know I was an adult, but having to explain after everything that had happened wasn't easy. I walked slowly downstairs and very carefully lifted my keys before silently unlocking the front door, and as soon as I closed it, I ran to my car so I could quickly drive off. My foot was shaking on the gas pedal and the thirty-minute drive seemed like it lasted forever. As soon as I pulled into Kaiden's driveway, again, something just didn't feel right. I ignored it and made my way inside, where the front door was unlocked.

"Kaiden," I called out.

I continued walking to find him standing in the living room with his arms crossed and a neutral expression on his face. He didn't greet me like he used to, which was strange. Something was wrong, and I was going to find out.

"Is everything okay?"

His finger started tapping on his crossed hand and when he had uncrossed his arms, I flinched for some odd reason.

"I don't know, Hailey. You tell me."

I took his appearance in and noticed he was wearing the same outfit the night I found out what he does. There was a splatter of blood on him and the air suddenly grew thick.

"What do you mean? What's going on? Why are you even dressed like that?"

I guess my words set him off. His eyebrows furrowed and his mouth turned into a scowl.

"That's not really any of your business, and don't try to change the subject."

"I wasn't trying to change the subject. And there's no need to be rude."

The room turned cold and the hairs on the back of my neck stuck up as soon as I heard footsteps behind me.

"What's going on?"

I turned around to find Hunter there wearing some dark and suspicious clothing too, and now this felt like a setup.

However, Hunter was as confused as me, so that strangely calmed me down a tad bit.

"Now that you're both here. Is there anything you two would like to tell me?"

All I could think of was he knew.

I looked at Hunter and back at Kaiden, and the scowl turned into full-blown rage.

"I don't know what you're talking about." Hunter said.

It's stupid of me to say. I was trying to deflect, but it was denial that this was actually happening.

"Tell me what the fuck is going on?" He asked.

But each word was emphasized. Hunter tried to play stupid, but Kaiden wasn't having it. Seeing him mad when his mom died was one thing, but this was another level of hurt. His hand started a motion like he was trying not to blow up.

"Why the fuck did you pin Hailey against my door earlier?"

Okay, maybe he didn't know. Is what I was trying to tell myself. This couldn't be happening, but that's the thing with secrets. The truth always comes to light in the end.

"What is going on between you two, huh?"

My mouth was frozen. I couldn't speak or even breathe. This wasn't happening. I should've never left the house. I exchanged looks with Hunter and literally begged him not to say anything, even when there was no denying it any longer. But I wasn't ready yet.

"I guess there is no use in keeping it from him anymore." He finally spoke.

"What the hell are you talking about?" Kaiden yelled.

I stared at Hunter with tears in my eyes. Begging him not to.

"Are you going to tell him, or should I?" Hunter asked me.

Why is he doing this to me? Why am I the only one freaking out? He was so nonchalant, as if he didn't care what happens.

"Somebody better start fucking talking before I lose it. Tell me what the fuck is going on between the two of you!"

But I was stuck. I went to open my mouth, but nothing came out. I started shaking my head as he kept asking me to tell him. Over and over and my head was starting to explode.

"I SLEPT WITH HUNTER!"

Chapter 21

"What the hell did you just say?" Kaiden asked.

The room went quiet, and for the first time, the world went silent. My hands were on my head as the ringing feeling was back. I couldn't look him in the eyes, but a part of me felt a weight lift off my shoulders. Carrying this secret was the worst thing, but the look on Kaiden's face was even worse. Yet he was so calm, and that was scarier.

"You're joking, right? Tell me this is a fucking joke."

But silence spoke louder than words. I looked at Hunter, and for the first time, shame was written all over his face.

"Hunter, you better tell me this is a fucking joke. Say it's a joke!"

His head fell and Hunter was running his hands through his hair.

"I wish it was a joke. But it's not."

His words were so soft, but those words cut Kaiden deep.

"We were drunk, Kaiden. We weren't thinking clearly." I tried to soften the blow.

"You slept with my best friend, Hailey. My fucking best friend! Of all the men you could've chosen, you had to pick my best friend!"

"Chose? It wasn't planned. It just happened."

I reached for his arm, but he snatched it away from me.

"You still did it! I knew you were naive, but I didn't think you were stupid. . ."

Here is where the mean Kaiden comes back. I deserved it. I probably deserve a hell of a lot worse, too.

"I was drunk, and I was sad after you left me. I didn't think, and he was there for me. He treated me with kindness. It just happened. But I didn't do it to intentionally hurt you."

"I was a goddamn mess! I just buried my fucking mother and was a fucking wreck! Don't you dare try to say this is my fault!" Kaiden yelled.

He walked over to Hunter, leaving my sight.

"And you. You were supposed to be my best friend. How could you do this to me? You fucking knew what she meant to me!"

Kaiden's anger took over as he pulled the gun from the back of his pants and aimed it at Hunter. Kaiden has always said he would die for me. That he would hurt anyone who tried to hurt me and I never took him seriously. Until now.

"Put the gun down, Scott."

I was clung to the wall, watching it all unfold between my eyes. Hunter was standing there with no hint of emotion in his eyes while the barrel of the gun was inches from his face. Did I do this? Did one moment manage to change everything that I knew? And was it worth it? Kaiden's hand was shaking and you could see the rage in his eyes as tears fought their way out.

"You were my best friend! Was this your plan all along?" He yelled out.

But how was Hunter so calm? Like it wasn't the first time with a gun in his face. I was terrified for him.

"What the hell are you talking about?" Hunter asked, sounding slightly annoyed.

I wanted to move or just say something, but the shock took over my body and I somewhat couldn't do any of it.

"Admit it!" Kaiden yelled again.

He had cocked the gun, leaving just a soft touch before it fires. Why wasn't Hunter reacting?

"Be careful with the gun, Scott. One wrong move and someone could get hurt."

With a quick movement, Kaiden suddenly had his arm to Hunter's chest and the gun to his face. I looked at him with shock and fear. I'd never seen him like this before. I had to do something. But what could I possibly do?

"Shoot me, go ahead. And make sure you don't miss. Because if you do. . ." Hunter grunted, "you earn an enemy and you should know you don't want me as one."

Was I stupid? At this moment, I was. I placed myself in front of Hunter. He didn't deserve to die because I made the decision. I could've said no. He asked me three times, and I said yes. Kaiden was shocked when I moved in front of him, but he immediately retracted.

"Are you fucking insane? I could've shot you!"

He relaxed and took a deep breath.

"If anyone deserves that bullet. It's me. Not him."

My red and teary eyes met his, which carried pain behind them.

"Just go. Get the hell out, both of you!"

"Kaiden, I—"

"I said get the hell out, Hailey. I never want to see you again!" He yelled.

"You don't mean that. Kaiden." I tried to hold back my tears.

"I mean it. Get the hell out now!"

I didn't fight this time. We hurt him, and he probably doesn't want anything to do with me after this. Hunter had left already, and I was following after him. Once the door closed, it all came down. I had no one to blame but myself. Did I really expect him to want anything to do with me after finding out I slept with his best friend? I managed to make it to my car, but the pain was overwhelming.

***

Hunter

I wouldn't show it. Show how much it sucked that I just lost my best friend today. Because I made a decision, I can't take back. If I was honest, I wouldn't take it back. I just wish it wasn't with my best friend's girl. Hailey made her way over to her car, but as soon as she got there, she broke down. Her body slid down against her car and her face was buried in her hands as she cried her heart out. I should walk away. Everything would be less complicated if I walked away, but I couldn't allow myself to do that. I left my car and went over to her.

"Are you okay?"

Stupid, stupid, stupid question, but wasn't sure what else to say. Her face was covered in tears and her hair was stuck to her face, but the moment I asked, she stood up and reflected all her anger on me.

"No, Hunter. I am not okay."

Her arms came flying at me as she shoved my shoulder, but it didn't even move me an inch.

"This is your fault!" She screamed.

"My fault? Weren't you just in there trying to take a bullet for me? Which, by the way, was very stupid of you."

She went back to shoving me a few more times before I got annoyed and grabbed both her wrists. She tried fighting against me before she stopped and lowered her head, sobbing. I finally released her arms.

"Go ahead. Blame it all on me. Whatever makes you feel better about yourself. Just remember, it takes two to tango."

Her hand went flying as it made its way across my cheek. Instant regret appeared on her face, but now I was pissed. I just laughed because I let her get away with way too much. I pulled her to her car and left her no room for her to escape.

"Hailey. Poor victim Hailey. She could never do anything wrong."

I wanted to teach her a lesson and I am not a person who handles conflict softly. I reached for my gun and held the barrel under her chin. She was scared, and she should be.

"I've already killed two people today. Lost my best friend, and now have been slapped. Don't make me want to kill one more."

But once again, I underestimated her. Hailey grabbed my hand and pressed the gun more on her skin.

"Then do it. You make so many threats that I actually want to see you do it. You want to do this instead of taking accountability like you had no part in it. So do it, because I promise you, this bullet will feel less painful than what just happened."

She finally snapped. I knew that's what was happening. The rage that ignited mixed in with the pain was enough to realize that life isn't what you want it to be. Her blue eyes stared directly into my soul, which made it hard not to admire.

"That's where you're wrong. I've been owning my mistakes, but apparently, it's just my fault. The fact is, you can't handle the truth. I also won't let you hit me whenever you feel like it."

"Oh, so you have to one-up me by pointing a gun at me?" She continued.

So-fucking-naive.

"Yeah, because you seem to lack boundaries. You've crossed mine and I've looked the other way too many times. I've had enough."

Her breathing accelerated, and she was starting to turn red from the anger. "Boundaries? You of all people are going to talk about boundaries? You don't give a shit about anyone but yourself! This whole being the nice guy until you get what you want! Not even caring if you'd hurt anyone! So, you either shoot me right now, or put the gun down because you're not scaring anyone, and I sure as hell am over your petty threats!"

The fearless and fire girl I knew was trapped in her. I knew deep down there was someone with a backbone ready to come out, and she had come in full force. The fact that she was always so calm and collected just seemed so unreal. Especially since our day. . . I remember everything and she took full control. When she told me she wanted me, I was selfish. Because I wanted her just as bad. Kaiden always said she was submissive, but that was not what I had experienced with her that day. So, the first taste I got, I didn't want it to end. I wanted more. There was no way that I was going to stop when she wanted me and everything she wanted to do. We did. It was like a burning desire that had been unleashed. Being challenged has never felt so damn amazing. So, I melted. I caved. My hand snaked around her waist as I pulled her into a heated kiss. My gun was still in my hand and resting on the other side of her head. I thought she would pull away, but she didn't.

    She didn't even flinch at the metal that rested on her head while I got a taste of her again. She was right about one thing, though. . . I didn't even think about the consequences. I had a soft spot for Hailey Davis, and she caught my bluff. Hailey melted into my hands and body, and it felt so damn right. I couldn't understand how something so wrong could feel so right at the same time. I clung to her, not knowing what the hell was going on or what she was doing to me. But quite frankly, I saw why two opposites attract. But then reality set in. What am I doing? We hadn't even left Kaiden's house yet, and I was kissing the girl he was in love with. She meant nothing to me, and I was throwing years of friendship away for some attraction. I had to pull away because this was so fucking wrong. But when I finally did. Her face was just as confused as mine. It wasn't just a fucking kiss. She's the reason I threw my morals and friendship out the door when I let the temptations in.

Him and I

***

Kaiden

But I saw it all. Beer in my mouth just watching them fight and when he kissed her. It was at this moment I didn't know Hailey at all. It was at this moment I saw a side of her I never knew existed. It was at this moment I realized I never knew her at all. The pain of knowing someone I loved for so long was capable of betraying me and then being able to apologize and then continue to betray me was a different level of pain. She was pain. I hated that after what she did. I still loved her. I fucking love this girl and she fucked my best friend. Hunter was my best friend, but he was not the kind of guy you settle down with. He is disrespectful toward women and the fact I didn't see it before that he would do that to someone like her. I never realized a lot of things. Seeing them kiss in front of my fucking eyes was insulting, but that's not what bothered me the most. It was the look in Hunter's eyes. I've never seen it before because they said it was a drunken mistake. The way he looked at her and kissed her told me that he was falling for her. I know that because she was the type of person who, when you finally have, you don't fuck it up. She was easy to fall for and I fucked that up. I drove her into another man's arms. So, I don't blame her more than I blame myself. I still loved her, though. I'll be damned if I allow him to be with her. I may be mad now, but she is the love of my life who made a mistake. Hell, I've treated her worse.

As far as for Hunter.

He was dead to me.

***

Hailey

But this wasn't the end. It was just the beginning of self-discovery. Hunter kissing me was shocking, but what was more shocking was that I liked it. I didn't want it to end. It wasn't like how you kiss someone you love. It was like when you kiss someone you hate, but you can't live without. I saw him in a different light, and it scared the living shit out of me to know that I did. My mother always told me to never fall for the guy who gives you butterflies. You fall for the one who makes you feel safe. But what about the one who sets your whole body on fire and likes you as your real self? What about the one who makes you angry but takes care of you at your worst? What about the one who allows you to be mad and never lets anger make you feel so small?

I never thought I'd be at a stage of my life where Kaiden isn't the only person in my heart. He was all I saw at first.

Now, with this kiss, I was confused. I was more than confused. Funny thing was, that wasn't the end of the story. This was a turning point and I wish I could say things got easier from here. Let's just say it's more complicated than that.

Acknowledgments

From the bottom of my heart, thank you to my amazing family and friends who had my back throughout my writing journey. Thanks to my love for writing, I have made friendships that will last a lifetime, and I couldn't be more grateful for that. And most importantly, to all of my readers from Episode who did nothing but support me, motivating me to keep writing. And to all my readers here, for choosing my book and sticking to the end. Thank you, my dearest reader!

About the Author

Melia A has loved to write stories since she was a little girl. As she grew older, she started playing interactive games. At first, she was only a reader, but gradually she learned how to create interactive stories herself. It became her passion, which then turned into her full-time job. Currently, she has culminated over 50 million reads on Episode app, and all of her stories became successful, winning millions of hearts of worldwide. After being inspired to do so by her readers, she decided to convert and publish her most frequently read story into a book. Him and I is the first book in this series, and it marks her debut as a novelist. She lives in a charming city of Sweden, and whenever she's not writing, she loves to read steamy stories full of drama.

Printed in Great Britain
by Amazon